Praise for *Sir Fig Newton and the Science of Persistence*:

"A noteworthy debut." —*Kirkus Reviews*, starred review

"Middle grade readers looking for realistic stories with engaging protagonists will enjoy meeting Mira, a girl whose passion for science gives her a sense of purpose and the tools to solve problems." —*SLJ*

A 2022 Oregon Spirit Book Award Honor

A 2023 Oregon Book Award finalist for the Leslie Bradshaw Award for Middle Grade and Young Adult Literature

An Oregon Center for the Book 2023 National Book Festival Children's selection

A 2023 Washington State Book Award Finalist

A Bank Street Best Book of the Year

Also by Sonja Thomas:

Sir Fig Newton and the Science of Persistence

Olive Blackwood
TAKES
ACTION!

SONJA THOMAS

ALADDIN

NEW YORK LONDON TORONTO SYDNEY NEW DELHI

ALADDIN

An imprint of Simon & Schuster Children's Publishing Division

1230 Avenue of the Americas, New York, New York 10020

First Aladdin hardcover edition May 2024

Text copyright © 2024 by Sonja Thomas

Jacket illustration copyright © 2024 by Simone Douglas

All rights reserved, including the right of reproduction in whole or in part in any form.

ALADDIN and related logo are registered trademarks of Simon & Schuster, LLC.

Simon & Schuster: Celebrating 100 Years of Publishing in 2024

For information about special discounts for bulk purchases, please contact Simon & Schuster Special Sales at 1-866-506-1949 or business@simonandschuster.com.

The Simon & Schuster Speakers Bureau can bring authors to your live event. For more information or to book an event contact the Simon & Schuster Speakers Bureau at 1-866-248-3049 or visit our website at www.simonspeakers.com.

Designed by Tiara Iandiorio

The text of this book was set in Adobe Garamond Pro.

Manufactured in the United States of America 0424 BVG

10 9 8 7 6 5 4 3 2 1

CIP data for this book is available from the Library of Congress.

ISBN 9781665939331 (hc)

ISBN 9781665939355 (ebook)

For Mom

Chapter One

Voilà! Our Spell Is Done

FADE IN:

EXTERIOR OLIVE'S BACKYARD. DAY.

Fully fenced backyard of charming bungalow house nestled in an urban neighborhood lined with tall

trees. CLOSE-UP of OLIVE holding
an opened velvet bag. KAYLA
digs her gloved hand inside and
pulls out rose-colored marbles.
They both lay the marbles one by
one in the grass, preparing for
their "Reveal It Now" spell.

> OLIVE (VOICE-OVER)
> My best friend, Kayla,
> and I always do our
> best to follow the
> rules of magic. One
> of those rules, and my
> favorite, is that Magic
> Is Stronger When Done
> Together.

A winter chill hugged the air, but Olive didn't mind. She preferred doing spells outside when no one was around. And as usual, Mom was still at work. But even more important, Olive was on a super-important mission.

Today she would choose the perfect story for her next film.

"Any ideas yet?" Kayla asked.

Olive pushed up her red glasses. "Still thinking." She shrugged.

There were several loglines bouncing around in her head:

- A reimagining of *The Witches*, where a young kid stumbles onto a wizarding convention and must save the good witches from their evil grandmother, even after being turned into a cat.

- A silent Halloween dinner with a daughter and her deceased father, when suddenly they're ambushed by candy corn–eating zombies.

- When a bully unleashes a destructive spell on a middle school, timid thirteen-year-old twins must step up to save their classmates.

But Olive wasn't ready to say them out loud yet. Before sharing, she wanted to choose her favorite one with 100 percent confidence. Even when sharing with her best friend.

"I have the perfect film for you," Kayla said.

Olive plucked another marble from the bag. "Yeah?"

"Nick and James claim that there are R.A.A.T.S. roaming the park near our neighborhood."

Olive paused. "Say, huh?"

"R.A.A.T.S. Rodents at a tremendous size." Kayla rolled the few marbles she had left in her hand. "You could do one of those found-footage movies. A town invaded by gigantic radioactive rats!"

Kayla's older twin brothers were always making up ridiculous stories. But it could make an interesting film. It reminded Olive of the R.O.U.S.—rodents of unusual size. These giant ratlike creatures live in fire swamps in one of her dad's favorite fantasy films from decades ago, *The Princess Bride.*

Olive mentally added it to her list.

She dropped the last marble to the ground and stepped back. Their large circle was complete! They interlocked their right pinkie fingers and chanted in unison, "This is just between us." Dancing around the marbles, the two sang:

"Hocus-pocus!
Bring in focus,
the film that should be done.

Boom, boom, kapow!
Let us know now,
the film that should be done."

Kayla shimmied gracefully. Olive awkwardly bounced along. They continued moving around the circle until they'd repeated the verses three times, and then ended with:

"Presto! Shazam!
Alakazam!
Voilà! Our spell is done."

Turning thirteen in April, Olive would finally be able to attend the Rose City Summer Film Camp. Ten lucky students would get to produce a short film, from developing the screenplay to final editing. Rumors buzzed that Gillian Vansant would be a guest speaker this summer. She'd attended the camp as a kid and recently got nominated for Best Director at the Oscars!

Getting into Rose City would be a huge step toward making Olive's directorial dreams come true. The most important part of the application was to submit an eight-minute short. And that was exactly why Olive was doing this spell.

"Well?" Kayla said.

Olive still wasn't sure which story to pick. But she did know the perfect location to film it. "Off to the cemetery!"

Olive wasn't allowed to wander in the nearby park after dark, even if she wasn't alone. Luckily, there was still an hour before sunset. That would give Olive and Kayla enough time to take the unfamiliar path on their way to the cemetery with the hopes of spotting R.A.A.T.S.

Though Olive doubted that the twins' story about rodents at a tremendous size was true, it couldn't hurt to make a quick investigation. Who knew what interesting footage she might capture?

At the edge of the park, Olive and Kayla stepped off the sidewalk and into a thick patch of trees. They zigged and zagged, stepping over roots, and avoiding low-hanging branches. Olive held her phone above her feet. With each heavy stomp, her winter boots snapped twigs and crunched leaves. She panned the phone toward the towering conifers and redwoods blocking out the sun. Deeper in, the usual neighborhood sounds faded.

Still filming, Olive asked, "Are you sure you know where we're going?"

Kayla nodded. "The twins gave me detailed directions."

Olive released a heavy sigh. She let her mind wander as it often did. Her best film ideas came to her this way. As she carefully stepped over another tree root, she imagined that this was the part in the movie where the best friends were separated. Her boot would get caught, causing her to fall and sprain her ankle. So the sidekick would have to go for help, leaving the injured hero alone in the woods to fend for herself. Against gigantic and *hungry* radioactive rats!

Something howled. Olive jumped, wobbling back into the present.

The trees had become sparser. Off in the distance a jogger was accompanied by a German shepherd. Olive laughed it off.

Kayla froze. "Did you hear that?"

Olive strained to listen. As she was shaking her head, a twig snapped.

Kayla's hand flew over her mouth. She pointed at something large and low to the ground.

Olive squinted, then jerked back.

A large humpbacked beast—at least three feet long—lumbered in the distance.

Was it . . . ? No, it couldn't be. Could it? There's no such thing as rodents at a tremendous size! Right?

Her fingers shaking, Olive swung her camera's view toward the moving creature. Kayla leaned into Olive. Their gazes locked onto the screen. Moving her hands to keep the fuzzy critter in frame, Olive zoomed in as far as her phone would allow. She gasped.

It had four huge chisel-shaped buckteeth! On top *and* bottom. And they were orange!

The beast growled. Kayla and Olive shrieked.

As it waddled on, Olive registered the creature's tiny, rounded ears and thick reddish-brown fur. Once she caught sight of its broad, flat tail, that's when she knew. She'd seen this animal on the back of the state flag since kindergarten. It also happened to be their middle school's mascot.

"It's a beaver!" Olive said.

"He's so cute," Kayla cooed.

Olive giggled. "It's definitely at a tremendous size."

"What should we call him? Justin Beaver?"

Olive groaned. "Butternut? Gnawly? Webber?"

Kayla shook her head with each one.

"I know," Olive said. "Waddle!"

Kayla made the heart hand sign.

Olive turned back to her phone's screen. "Hey, where's Waddle?"

They stared out into the distance, but their new friend was gone.

Chapter Two

Dying to Know

A MURDER OF CROWS lined along the wrought iron fence at the entrance into the Lone Fir Cemetery. Under other circumstances, Olive would've shivered in fright at the scene before her. The crows' beady eyes followed every move she and Kayla made. But Olive wasn't scared. She was focused on her mission. To choose the perfect story to film for her Rose City application.

Olive held up her phone, slowly panning over the long stretch of curious crows. She zoomed in until one of them filled the screen. The late-afternoon sunlight exposed brilliant metallic blues and greens hidden in the urban bird's black feathers.

As Olive zoomed back out, a gust of wind rustled the leaves of the towering trees. Kayla sneezed. With an annoyed burst of harsh caws, the crows took off.

With a loud sniff, Kayla wiped at her nose. "Sorry!"

"No worries. Catching the crows in flight was a cool shot."

The two headed through the open cemetery gate and wandered along the wide dirt path. Even on a cold Thursday in January, there was a handful of people strolling about. Most likely to soak up the unexpected sunshine before it faded away.

"So, where to?" Kayla asked.

"I'll know when we find it," Olive said, slowing her stride.

Most of the headstones were flat plaques. Every few rows, different shapes and sizes would stand out. Like a mini Washington Monument or a three-foot-long cylinder. Very few had flowers because so many had death dates in the late 1800s and early 1900s. There was even a big tomb and a mausoleum. But it was a cluster of family headstones that stopped Olive in her tracks.

"Whoa, look at that." She gestured at the grave marker. A color photo of a husband and wife eyed them back.

"Beevers." Kayla read the family surname out loud. "Ugh, how awful."

"I thought the name was kinda neat, especially after finding Waddle."

Kayla shook her head. The beads at the end of her box braids clicked together.

"Not that. The guy, Henry, is already dead, but his wife, Ellie, there's no date. How creepy to see your head-stone when you're still alive." Kayla shuddered.

"That's it!" Olive shot over to a gigantic tree several yards away. Kayla hustled close behind.

Olive patted the big-leaf maple's mossy bark. "This is the location."

"I'm dying to know." Kayla paused, trying to catch her breath. "What's your movie gonna be about?"

Olive grinned, and with 99.9 percent confidence declared, "A Halloween dinner. Like the kind your aunt T does with her kitchen-witch friends."

"Ooh, you mean a Dumb Supper," Kayla said, tapping her fingertips together. "Where they invite loved ones who've passed on and celebrate with a huge dinner, eating in silence."

Olive nodded.

A pagan celebration, Samhain began as a Celtic festival of the dead on Halloween. It's when the magical veil between the physical world and the spirit world was thin, giving people a chance to connect with the spirits of those who were gone.

"How come we've never tried it before?" Kayla asked.

"Because you can't keep quiet for five minutes, let alone an entire dinner!"

Kayla pursed her lips, then burst into giggles. "True, but it's hereditary."

Olive laughed in agreement. Kayla's family was so big and fun, they couldn't be contained in one house. Kayla lived with her parents and four older brothers in the big yellow house on Bucknell Place. Then there were both sets of grandparents, five uncles, seven aunts, and tons of cousins—as well as all the play cousins—who lived in Oregon or across the bridge in Washington. Olive couldn't imagine what it would be like to have such a huge family who hung out all the time. The thought made her twitch.

"Plus," Kayla said, "I'd rather dress up and dance."

This past Halloween was the first one they hadn't gone trick-or-treating. Some unspoken rule said it was too childish now that they were in the seventh grade. Though they still got to dress up for the school dance. Both had been witches from *The Wiz*. Kayla as Glinda the Good, and Olive as Evillene.

Olive frowned when she remembered how Kayla had kept bugging her to ask this cute boy to dance. Bobby Filmore was from their Spanish class, and she'd had a crush on him since sixth grade. Olive had kept making up excuses, but Kayla always had a comeback.

"Maybe he has a girlfriend," Olive had said.

"Nope, he doesn't," Kayla had replied.

"Maybe he hates dancing."

"Then why was he just dancing with his friends? Want me to ask for you?"

Maybe he thinks I'm gross and ugly and weird.

Olive had never said that one out loud. Though

she'd definitely believed it, along with a whole spiral of other negative thoughts. Instead, she'd said, "What if he says no?"

"What if he says yes?" Kayla had challenged. "You'll never know what will happen if you don't speak up."

What Kayla didn't seem to understand was that Olive was okay with liking Bobby from afar. Well, maybe not okay with it, but she'd accepted that she wasn't like Kayla. Smile? Say hello? Ask him to dance? No way! She winced as she pictured his response: laughing out loud.

Futuristic techno music blasted from a nearby apartment window and snapped Olive back into the present. A robotic voice belted out upbeat lyrics, the sound echoing around all the gravestones. Olive and Kayla looked at each other with raised brows. They exploded into giggles.

"Okay, wait, I've got the best idea," Kayla said. "I saw this old movie *Beetlejuice* with my family, and there's this hilarious scene where they're eating dinner. This ghost couple possesses all the guests because they want to get everyone out of their house. So the ghosts try to scare them by making them sing and dance."

"I love Tim Burton!"

Kayla looked confused, and Olive shook her head. "Never mind." She couldn't expect her best friend to remember every director who inspired her.

Olive quickly hit the record button on her phone as Kayla shuffled like a creepy zombie. Her head jerked toward her raised shoulder, then back, over and over. She shimmied and hopped, breaking into a sped-up version of Michael Jackson's "Thriller" dance.

A couple walking past gave Kayla a strange look. Olive could never put herself out there like that. But whenever Olive was behind a camera, it was like she had a magic shield protecting her from other's judgments and stares.

Olive zoomed in. She watched Kayla on the screen mouthing along with the thumping electronic music, her movements becoming more exaggerated. Once the song ended, Kayla dropped onto the grass, splayed out like a starfish.

She sat up excitedly. "I could choreograph the scene for you!"

Olive's head bobbed up and down. Taking her original idea and mashing it up with a fun ghost possession had her vibrating with excitement.

"And"—Kayla made jazz hands with wiggling fingers—"we could even get some of the girls from my dance team to be in it! You know Abigail would jump to be on film. And you've met Heather and April."

Olive's shoulders stiffened. Her enthusiasm vanished.

"With my choreography and your directing? You'll definitely get into film camp!"

Olive rubbed the back of her neck. "Yeah, sure, maybe."

But she could feel her skin grow hot. Directing girls from Kayla's dance team made it hard to breathe.

Control, Olive Blackwood. Must learn control.

She silently repeated the altered Yoda quote from *The Empire Strikes Back*. It was her way of trying to breathe normal again.

Kayla knew practically every secret, fear, and dream Olive had.

Olive's dream was to be an award-winning director of fantasy movies. Only Kayla knew that she used to include "world-famous" in her ambition too. Being allergic to attention—wanted or not—Olive had realized she'd rather the spotlight shine only on her work. Kayla understood that Olive hated speaking in front of an audience, no matter how small. That the very thought of being the center of attention made rashes sneak all over Olive's skin.

So why was Kayla nudging her past her comfort zone?

Hopefully, if Olive never mentioned it again, Kayla would forget all about her offer and Olive could make the film she'd already had in mind. A Silent Supper with just her, Dad, and zombies.

Chapter Three

A Sad Accordion

OLIVE'S TOP-THREE SCHOOL PERIODS were film, lunch, and Spanish. Film because, well, duh, it's film! The other two were the only periods she had with Kayla. Plus, who wouldn't enjoy staring at the supercute Bobby Filmore while learning to conjugate verbs like "gustar"?

But so far, her day wasn't going great.

First, she'd overslept and missed the school bus. Mom had already left for work. So Olive had to brave the TriMet bus alone.

She'd been squished between adults in suits and passengers in grungy clothing carrying bags of empty soda cans. Most appeared to be talking to themselves. Though the suits wore earbuds. The only positive was that Olive had imagined a great film scene. When a city bus gets hit with a meteorite, all the people on board can now talk to ghosts! With one exception. Thanks to her superpowered glasses, Olive could see them too!

At school, Mr. Ference had called on her twice in science. Both times he'd asked her to repeat herself because he couldn't understand her mumbling. Then she'd tripped in the halls—right in front of Bobby Filmore!

Unfortunately, lunch was just as unbearable. And there were still thirty minutes to go.

Kayla was going on nonstop about choreographing Olive's film. She'd already narrowed down a list of songs to her top three and put together a photo collage of possible outfits. Olive had tried twice to state her case that she didn't need the dance team's help. Both times she'd chickened out. Kayla was so excited to help her. Olive didn't want to hurt her feelings. She also didn't want to admit the reason why.

"Nothing too fancy," Kayla said. "I mean, yeah, it's a Silent Supper, so it's a super-important event, but there's the whole 'dining with the dead' mood to consider."

Olive's gaze wandered as Kayla gushed on. She began reading the posters on the lunchroom walls.

KEEP CASCADIA MIDDLE SCHOOL BEAUTIFUL: COMPOST AND RECYCLE

SMOKEY SAYS . . . ONLY YOU CAN PREVENT FOREST FIRES

Olive's eyes lingered on the black bear wearing a ranger hat and jeans. She'd never been camping before. Any interest had gone up in smoke after the terrifying wildfires that had started Labor Day weekend two years ago. Hearing about wildfires wasn't new. But experiencing some of the effects while it had happened had made it all too real.

The air had been so thick with smoke and ash, it had been impossible to see beyond a few feet. Olive could feel her throat tighten as she remembered it creeping into the house, making it hard to breathe. So many homes throughout Oregon had been destroyed. People had even died.

Before a whirlwind of catastrophic thoughts could take hold, Olive moved on to the next posters.

WANNA DANCE WITH SOMEBODY?
VALENTINE'S DANCE, FEBRUARY 19

CAFETERIA RULES: BE KIND. USE QUIET
VOICES. BE HONEST.

Be honest, Olive thought. Clearing her throat, she decided to try one more time.

"You know, I've been thinking . . ." Olive bit her bottom lip, searching for the right words without admitting her fear of directing Kayla's friends.

"Wait, you're gonna love this." Kayla held up both palms. "Since we don't want the vibe too somber either, because it *is* a celebration, after all, instead of wearing all black, each guest wears only one bold color! I'll be in gold. Abigail loves hot pink. . . ."

Olive took a crinkle-cut fry and stirred a dollop of mayo into the thick lump of ketchup on her lunch tray. She tried to keep calm and ignore the flutter building in her chest. Staring at her fries, Olive remembered reading somewhere why crinkle-cuts exist. Their unique wavy shape created more surface to fry, making them crispier than shoestring and waffle fries. So she never understood why every time the school served them, they were limp like a sad accordion.

"Hello-o, calling Olive Blackwood." Kayla nudged Olive's tray. "Did you hear me?"

Avoiding eye contact, Olive kept swirling the mayo-ketchup dip until it made a pleasing pink blob. She released a heavy sigh and dragged her gaze to meet Kayla's.

"Sorry, it's just that—

"I DON'T UNDERSTAND WHY IT'S SO HARD TO MAKE DECENT VEGAN MEALS!" Jo Willems's voice bellowed at the poor lady trying to ring them up at the register. Their voice wasn't so loud that it disrupted the entire cafeteria, but still intense enough that the students nearby were shaken. Even the lunch staff dishing out the food all took a step back.

The lunchroom monitor swooped in to defuse the situation. But it was clear from the heated conversation that Jo was refusing to back down.

"Whoa," Kayla said. "Jo has definitely made it their mission to veganize the school."

"And someday, the world," Olive joked.

The two cracked up, and Olive took the opportunity to switch the subject to anything far away from her film. Like weekend plans. And for almost ten minutes, Olive started to relax. Until Kayla abruptly stopped talking about her family's Friday-night itinerary.

Olive followed Kayla's widened gaze. Abigail Spencer was rushing over to their table. David Moore was coming in from the opposite direction. Before there was a chance to give warning, Abigail and David collided. David stumbled backward. His brown-bag lunch fell by Kayla's foot with a *splat*.

"Ugh, watch where you're going," Abigail huffed.

"Sorry." David took a step back, nodding as if he'd been at fault. He waved at Olive and Kayla. Olive waved back with a sympathetic smile.

She'd known David since kindergarten, and he was supersweet. Twice in gym he'd picked Olive for his volleyball team even though she stunk at sports. What a relief to *not* be the last one standing. He'd also helped her understand how to write an inequality using variables to solve "real-world" math problems. Like she cared whether she made enough cookies to feed at least fifty guests.

But people were always overlooking David. He was average height and size with regular brown hair and matching bland brown eyes. No freckles. No glasses. No braces. Not even a cool scar. Nothing about him stood out. He even wore the typical beige cargo pants and Oregon State tee. David didn't so much blend in as he completely disappeared.

"Here you go." Kayla held out David's semi-squashed bag.

He took it with a heartfelt "Thanks," then wandered off.

"Who was that weirdo?" Abigail said.

Drawing out the vowels in her name, Kayla replied, "Aaabbiii" in that don't-be-so-mean tone.

Olive frowned. "He's not . . ." Abigail's brow lifted in surprise. Olive could feel her armpits getting sweaty. "He's David, from film class."

"Whatever." She rolled her eyes and then planted both palms onto the lunchroom table. "Kayla, have you heard? Cindy's moving away."

Abigail's eyes sparkled, but Olive had no idea why this was such major news.

"Coach is going to have the team pick a new dance cocaptain!"

"That's awesome!" Kayla said. "Looks like we both have squad news today."

Abigail tilted her head in confusion.

"Olive's doing a short film, and I agreed to be the choreographer. Getting some of the girls to be in it would be perfect!"

Olive's jaw dropped.

Abigail squealed. "Ooh, what kind of dance? What about outfits? I have the cutest pink sequined dress."

Kayla filled Abigail in on the dinner scene from the old movie and the songs and outfits she had in mind. Olive didn't hear any of it. It was too hard to concentrate on anything except her pounding chest.

Olive picked up another crinkle-cut fry and resumed stirring her mayo-ketchup blob. Thanks to all her hesitating, she'd missed her opportunity. She knew exactly what it felt like to be limp like a sad accordion. Weak and silent.

Chapter Four

Documentary, My Dear Olive

WHY DID KAYLA HAVE to tell Abigail? *I never said I was going to cast the dance team. Now they've hijacked my film. I should've said something. Anything! Why didn't I say no in the first place?*

Olive edged through the crowded school hallway, unable to escape her spiraling thoughts.

Now I'm trapped. Sure, Kayla's only trying to help. But I wish she wouldn't.

Thankfully, it was the last period of the day. Film was

the one class where Olive felt most comfortable, even if she didn't talk much.

Mr. Dodd leaned against his desk, greeting every student as they made their entrance. Some walked in with a confident strut or animated flair. Some walked in with a hurried "please-don't-notice-me" gait. Olive fell into that last camp.

In a singsong voice, Mr. Dodd said, "Happy Friday, Olive!"

"Hey." She gave a slight nod while pushing up her glasses and slipped into her seat in the back of the room.

Mr. Dodd not only taught the beginning and advanced film electives but also sixth- and seventh-grade English. Pretty much every student knew him. And everyone loved him. Incredibly goofy, Mr. Dodd always wore a cheesy bow tie and matching suspenders. Today's eye-rolling pattern? Bow-tie pasta. He also cracked awful dad jokes and had messy hair. Olive often wondered if he did anything to it or if he just rolled out of bed and let his hair do its own thing.

Abigail dashed into the room as the final bell rang.

"Just in time," Mr. Dodd said.

"Wouldn't miss this class for anything," Abigail cooed, sliding into her seat next to Olive. She flashed Olive a look that read "Whew, that was close," while her hands wiggled an imaginary bow tie.

"How does Darth Vader like his toast?" Mr. Dodd paused. "On the dark side."

Groans filled the classroom except for a booming snort-laugh to Olive's right. She caught an actual grin on Jo's face, as bright as their neon shirt.

Someone said in a deep voice, "Luke, I'm your father."

"Actually, it's 'No, I *am* your father,'" said Esme.

Trying hard to repress a grin, Mr. Dodd wrote two words on the dry-erase board: *represent* and *re-present*. He turned back around to face the class, pausing with raised brows. He was all about dramatic suspense, both in movies and in real life.

"Now, who can tell me what the word 'represent' means?"

Olive slumped in her chair, hoping to avoid his hopeful gaze. Just the thought of speaking in class made red splotches creep up her brown skin on both sides of her face.

"Anyone?" Mr. Dodd asked again.

"When something stands for something else," Esme piped up. "Like how an angel on someone's shoulder represents the right choice and the devil on the other is the wrong one."

"Great visual example and a plot device often seen in cartoons," Mr. Dodd said. "What else?"

"All the different referee hand signals in sports, like . . . *safe!*" Jo shouted. They demonstrated the gesture, extending both arms out in front and then sweeping their arms out to their sides, palms down.

"There's all kinds of symbols on sheet music," Abigail chimed in.

"Or the elements on the periodic table."

"What the government's supposed to do for the people."

Different examples continued to flood the room. Mr. Dodd sailed back and forth in front of the class, his head nodding along with each response. Once the answers dried up, he came to a halt.

"How about the other word, 're-present'?" He pointed at the board.

Students shifted in their seats but remained silent.

"David?" Mr. Dodd called. "Why not take a stab at it?"

"Umm . . ." David's brows shot up, yet he grinned as if he was happy, maybe even a bit surprised, that Mr. Dodd had called on him. "Presenting something again?"

"Yes!" Mr. Dodd said. "Like a reenactment of something that has already happened. Or even presenting in a different way."

"Like when a book's made into a movie?" Esme suggested.

"Exactly," Mr. Dodd said. He returned to the board and wrote in large letters the words *opinion versus fact*. Before he could turn around, voices fired away.

"Point of view."

"Rumors."

"Hypothesis."

Mr. Dodd's smile grew brighter with each answer. "And what about 'fact'?"

The truth, the whole truth, and nothing but the truth streamed through Olive's mind, followed by the sound of a judge's gavel striking a sound block. Probably because her mom was a family attorney who loved to argue both inside and outside the courtroom.

Olive hung her head low, letting her corkscrew curls shield her face.

"It means it really happened," David said.

"Reality TV," Abigail muttered. Several students snickered. With a smug grin, she ran her hand through her blond hair, bringing attention to the chunky pink streaks underneath.

"Can a film have both 'opinions' and 'facts' in it?" Mr. Dodd asked.

"Well, yeah," Esme said. "They do all the time."

"And what does that look like?" Mr. Dodd asked.

"It's like this movie I recently saw with my dad," Jo said. "The one about that baseball player, Jackie Robinson. It's based on real events, but it's not a hundred percent accurate."

"How so?" Mr. Dodd pressed.

Jo scrunched up their face like they were trying to come up with the right answer. "Sometimes a scene shows what *might* have happened, like making up the dialogue."

"Movies also make the truth interesting by how they show it," Esme added. "If the director doesn't like Jackie Robinson, they could focus on something that makes him seem like a bad guy."

"I'm quite impressed, class." Mr. Dodd grabbed a stack of papers from his desk and started handing them out to the first person in each row. "We're going to spend the next month doing a fun group project on documentaries."

Whining grumbled through the room.

"All right, calm down." Mr. Dodd chuckled. "You don't have to make a full documentary, only a trailer."

Olive sighed heavily through her nose. She'd been hoping that they'd make a tribute to their favorite film genre or director. She'd even rather write a report on the history of film. A group project on documentaries was *not* going to make her directorial dreams come true. Gillian Vansant never *had* to make a boring documentary!

"To make the project more fun, I'm going to raise the stakes. Some of you may be familiar with the Rose City Summer Film Camp."

Olive sat up straight. Yes, she was *very* familiar.

"Spots are limited and competitive," Mr. Dodd continued. "But it's a wonderful way to get hands-on experience with cinema cameras and video-editing equipment.

"I'd love to see you all apply for this amazing opportunity. So, for extra encouragement, I'm offering the group with the highest score to have me personally pass along your trailer to the camp's head director, along with a written recommendation!"

Excited chatter filled the room.

Olive grinned.

After such a horrible day, *this* was the kind of good fortune Olive had been hoping for.

Mr. Dodd's recommendation could be her golden ticket to Rose City.

Chapter Five

Golden Raspberry

OLIVE BOUNCED IN HER seat as she imagined herself at film camp making movies with cinema cameras, lighting equipment, and boom mics! Once the excited chatter in the classroom died down, Mr. Dodd continued.

"I'll assign everyone to groups of three. Each group will put together a written plan and film a trailer for their documentary."

Abigail motioned at Olive and herself and then held up both hands with crossed fingers. Olive didn't care either way. They only sat together because Abigail was friends with Kayla. And because Abigail wasn't friends with anyone else in class. In truth, Abigail wasn't all that friendly, period.

"My recommendation is no guarantee that you'll get in," Mr. Dodd warned. "You'll still need to fill out the application and follow the submission guidelines. But it can go a long way into moving you ahead of the pack.

"To make it fair, the topic will be the same for everyone. A documentary about the school cafeteria."

Groans rumbled through the room.

"Now, before making judgments," Mr. Dodd said, "there are lots of famous food documentaries to sink your teeth into. Like *Cowspiracy* and *Jiro Dreams of Sushi*. Plus, it doesn't have to be about food. Each group can choose to focus on whatever they want, so get creative. As long as it has something to do with the lunchroom."

Olive scanned the handout. Her back stiffened.

Next to the date "Thursday, February 17"—one month away—the word "PRESENTATION" loomed at her.

The last time Olive had spoken in front of a class, her

hands had gotten all clammy and her mouth had gone dry. She'd frozen, unable to finish.

"The best part?" Mr. Dodd tugged on his suspenders. "Teams will present their trailer at an evening assembly for the entire school! With teachers, students, and their parents!"

Olive's cheeks sizzled.

In front of the whole school? And parents?

That was a thousand times worse than only the class.

"It'll be a fun event with the cooking club providing refreshments and the school newspaper covering the festivities. Also, all attendees will vote on their favorite trailer." Mr. Dodd paused as the room filled with enthusiastic murmurs.

Abigail squealed. "I bet they'll take photos! I need to get a new outfit."

Olive nodded, but she didn't care about a possible photo opportunity. She just wanted to go to film camp. But speaking—in front of the *entire* school—had fear gnawing at her insides.

"I'll take the votes into consideration," Mr. Dodd said, "but I'll have final say on which team did the best on both the written plan and trailer. That team will receive my personal recommendation."

Mr. Dodd continued on, going into more detail about the project. But the moment he said "speech," Olive tuned him out, silently repeating, *Control. Control. Control.*

"Okay." Mr. Dodd cleared his throat. "The moment you've all been waiting for . . ." He shuffled through the papers on his desk until he found a small notebook. "The first team is . . ."

Please, please, please, put Esme and me in the same group, Olive prayed.

"Latesha, Audrey, and Wilder!"

Olive let out a shaky laugh.

In her opinion, Esme and she were both excellent filmmakers.

Esme's commercial last semester on the Portland Japanese Garden was amazing! Using seamless editing on her montage, the film showed all the different activities that happened during the weekend-long Lunar New Year celebration, from lantern-viewing to the traditional lion-dance performance.

Olive's commercial on the Witch's Castle in Forest Park wasn't so bad either. Mr. Dodd had called it eerie and unique. That was exactly the feel she was going for with the creepy organ music added in, using black-and-white film, and zooming in on a salamander inching past.

Paired with Esme, there's no way she would fail!

"Next up," Mr. Dodd continued, "is Esme, Jonathon—"

Olive sucked in her breath.

"—and Abigail."

All her air wheezed out.

Abigail shrugged at Olive with a pouty look.

Olive couldn't believe it! Abigail didn't even like making movies! And now she was in the same group as Esme? Abigail had only taken the class because she'd heard it was an easy A. And because Mr. Dodd was adorkably cute.

No, Olive argued with her nerves. *I'm not gonna lose this opportunity.*

There were still good filmmakers left. She could still win. She just had to!

Mr. Dodd continued reading. With each name called, Olive's heart pounded harder and faster. She could barely hear his voice with the rhythmic thumping in her ears.

With two groups left to announce, Mr. Dodd called, "Olive, David, and . . ." He squinted at his notebook. "Ah yes. Olive, David, and Jo!"

Olive's toes curled. She'd been paired with the two worst students in class! Now she'd never beat Esme.

David would never hurt anybody—not even a R.A.A.T.S. And nobody had ever said a bad thing about him. But that was the problem. No one ever said *anything* about David. Like his looks and style, his films were forgettable. Olive couldn't even remember what his commercial had been about!

And then there was Jo. They were loud in every way, from the colors they wore to their stubborn opinions. Their round face, often fierce and challenging, was topped off with short, spiky hair. Their films were just as pushy, like their commercial on being vegan. Talk about opinions! It made you feel that if you had one bite of a hamburger, then you were evil and destroying the planet.

Olive couldn't even imagine talking to Jo, let alone making a trailer with them.

"On Monday, your group will start brainstorming the focus of your project," Mr. Dodd said. "But for the rest of the period, we'll watch some documentary clips and trailers and discuss the most common characteristics."

The room darkened. A video about climate change with somber music played on the screen. Olive's thoughts wandered.

She believed that Mr. Dodd's endorsement would be that extra oomph to help get her into Rose City. Olive believed even more that the only award her partners' films would ever win was a Golden Raspberry, a parody award honoring the *worst* of cinematic under-achievements.

How in the world would Olive wow everyone at the assembly now? With Jo and David as her teammates, impressing that silly bow tie off Mr. Dodd was going to be impossible.

Chapter Six

Out of Focus

OLIVE TWISTED AND TURNED, trying to get comfortable on the stiff couch.

Living room, Olive thought with a loud snort. Filled with fancy furniture and framed reprints by long-dead artists, the room was so spotless that it felt more like a museum.

With one last pillow fluff, Olive gave up. She resumed watching her dad's favorite movie from when he was her age, *The NeverEnding Story*.

Olive loved Friday nights best when she spent them with Kayla. The two had met on their first day of kindergarten. She'd thought Kayla was the most interesting person in her class. Kayla's braids had been gathered into a faux-hawk, and she'd worn a pink tutu with rainbow boots.

During recess, their class had played duck, duck, goose, and Olive was "it." She'd tapped Kayla's shoulder when calling out "Goose!" But instead of chasing Olive, Kayla had grabbed Olive's hand and led her in a silly dance.

"You're funny!" Olive had giggled.

"You're fun!" Kayla had shrieked.

The two had been inseparable ever since.

Unfortunately, tonight her best friend was out doing some fun family thing. Again. One of Kayla's relatives always had a graduation, anniversary, or birthday to celebrate.

Olive didn't have any siblings. It was only her and Mom.

Munching on popcorn, Olive tried to escape into the movie's world of Fantasia. She imagined herself as Atreyu, a young warrior tasked with saving the world from the Nothing. Though deep down she realized that she was more like the shy Bastian character, hiding in the pages of a book. Or, in her case, behind a camera.

Olive leaned forward. It was the first Ivory Tower scene, and one of her favorites. Hidden in the crowd of Fantasians were Yoda, Chewbacca, Ewoks, and C-3PO. But Olive was out of focus. Her thoughts kept replaying Mr. Dodd calling out "Olive, David, and Jo."

Suddenly, keys jingled in the front door. A few seconds later, Olive's mom bustled inside carrying a satchel and two boxes. Her heeled boots clacked against the wood floors. She set the boxes down and dropped her keys onto the side table with a loud *clank*.

"No Kayla tonight?" Mom asked, followed with a kiss on top of Olive's head.

Catching a whiff of citrus perfume, Olive scrunched her nose. "Nope. Another family celebration."

Mom laughed. "Why am I not surprised?"

Olive's eyes remained on the TV screen. Her tongue poked at a popcorn kernel stuck in her teeth.

"Ooh, *The NeverEnding Story*? I love this movie!"

Mom said, removing her gloves and winter coat. "I wish I could join you, but—"

"I know." Olive rolled her eyes. "You got a big case for an important client and gotta work late."

"Sweetie." Mom sighed. "You know it takes a lot of hard work to fight for these families. So yes, I'm working late, and you're on your own for dinner. There's leftover lasagna in the fridge."

Olive nodded and shoved a handful of popcorn into her mouth. Mom was always working long hours on some case for some *other* family. Other than their ritual Sunday-night dinner, Olive couldn't remember the last time they'd eaten together. They'd even missed having dinner on Olive's last birthday.

"Or you can order a pizza. I'd never turn down a slice from Pizza Schmizza."

Olive *loved* Pizza Schmizza. But they didn't have online ordering, and she hated calling strangers. She knew her fears were absurd. Olive sometimes even made fun of herself. What horrible thing could happen if she ordered a pepperoni pizza? It's not like they would laugh at her or ban her from ever ordering again.

Yet she couldn't make the call. It wasn't worth the anxiety-induced rash and belly butterflies.

Olive gave a slight shrug and continued eating popcorn.

"Oo-kaay." Mom drew out the word as if she didn't know what else to say. She ran a manicured nail through her relaxed hair. Finally, she added, "Have a good night."

Once again, she kissed Olive's head of tight curls, and Olive scrunched her nose in return. This time because of the over-the-top affection. Or maybe because once again they weren't sitting down to dinner like a normal family. Or more likely because Mom hadn't even asked her about her day. Weren't parents supposed to ask their kids things like "How was school?"

Olive couldn't stop obsessing over her documentary project. She really needed someone to talk to. But her best friend was busy. And Mom had more important things to do than fret about silly things. Things that mattered to Olive. Like unwanted teammates, personal recommendations, and presenting in front of the entire school.

Olive switched off the TV and headed to her room. There *was* one person Olive could always count on when she needed him.

Chapter Seven

Internet in Heaven

OLIVE CRASHED ONTO HER bed, tablet in hand. She opened the folder named "Dad" and clicked on the most recent file. A video of her father talking into the camera filled the screen. He had a friendly face with a large smile to match. His mustache and beard were slightly over-grown, but nowhere near hipster length. His short Afro hid underneath a black fedora, emblazoned with the words "Happy New Year."

"Hello, my beautiful Olive!"

Her shoulders relaxed.

"Many people make resolutions this time of year, but that was never my thing. Maybe because I have everything I ever wanted—you and your mom—so what else is there? But if making a list of what you want is something you like to do, then here's my advice.

"Go after whatever fills your heart with joy."

Wearing a big toothy grin, Dad lifted the fedora so he could wipe at his glistening dark skin.

"Then go after those things with everything you got. You're my baby girl, and I know you can do anything you put your heart and mind to."

Olive pursed her lips. He sounded like Kayla. She wondered how confident he'd be in his "baby girl" if he knew that she couldn't even make a simple call to order a pizza. Or tell her best friend the truth. That she didn't want Kayla's help.

"All right, you ready, Olive?"

The camera tilted down and zoomed in on Dad's watch. The second hand inched toward midnight.

"Ten. Nine. Eight . . ."

Olive didn't count along like she usually did. The

usual comfort from seeing her father was dimmed by her tingling unease.

"Two. One! Happy New Year!"

He blew into a horn and the curled-up paper tube unfurled with a *whuuhhmmpf* sound.

"Cheers to a year filled with laughs, hugs, and lots of love."

Olive's dad had died from multiple myeloma when she was six, but she still saw him all the time. A few days before her ninth birthday, Mom had sat her down.

"The moment your dad found out he was sick, he started recording messages for you," Mom had explained. "He still wanted to be in your life after he was gone. So he came up with the idea of scheduling emails to send his messages to you.

"I'm sure this is all confusing, but I don't want you to be afraid. It's just your daddy letting you know how much he loves you. Do you have any questions?"

Olive's only response had been "I didn't know they have Internet in heaven!"

She received a video every month, including on Halloween, Christmas, New Year's Day, Valentine's Day, and

April thirteenth, for her birthday. Sometimes, when Olive needed someone to talk to, she'd make a video message back to her father. Tonight was one of those times.

Sitting cross-legged on her bed, Olive pulled her curls into a loose bun. She took a deep breath and hit the record button.

"Hey, Dad." Her voice was small and shaky. "I know you said that I could do anything I put my mind to, but . . ."

Her gaze darted around the room and hesitated on the three framed movie posters displayed on her wall. They were Dad's from when he was growing up: *The NeverEnding Story*, *Time Bandits*, and *Star Wars*.

"But sometimes I'm not so sure."

She rambled on about her fears of not getting into film camp.

"Now Kayla's the choreographer, costume designer, *and* music supervisor. All I wanted was to film a silent dinner with you and me at the cemetery."

Olive could see the scene play out in her mind, Dad and her dining together in silence. First, she would film herself at the cemetery sitting by the big-leaf maple tree with Dad's favorite dishes spread out before her: barbe-cued ribs, greens, and corn bread. Using the green screen effect on her iMovie software, she'd overlay footage of her father from one of his videos onto hers. Then she'd decrease the color saturation to adjust Dad's image so he appeared cold like a ghost.

While enjoying their Halloween dinner, zombies would attack. Hopefully played by Kayla and her twin brothers. Stumbling toward them, the monsters would moan "Corn" instead of "Brains."

All Kayla's brothers, especially Nick and James, were like her brothers too. They all had appeared at least once in the fantasy movies she'd been making since the third grade. She'd have no problem directing them as hungry zombies.

Olive's smile disappeared as she remembered how her day had kept getting worse.

"Not only do I have lousy teammates, but we have to present our trailer in front of the whole school. What if I mess up? Like in social studies last year, when everyone laughed and I ended up with a B and ruined my 4.0 average."

Olive stopped the story there. She didn't want to share how she'd frozen and couldn't finish her speech on the Oregon Trail. Or how she'd bolted out of class with serious stomach cramps. Even worse, how she'd had her first diarrhea attack in public.

She'd begged Mrs. Tucker to let her do extra credit to no avail. Olive had even contemplated doing a spell to change Mrs. Tucker's mind. But the rules of magic stated that they should never be used to force someone's will. Even if that someone was a mean old teacher.

Dad would understand her desperate situation. He'd been a film major at Cal U near LA. He, too, wanted to make blockbuster fantasy films. Though, his personality had flourished under attention. Mom once laughed recalling how he'd dreamed of strutting down the red carpet with cameras flashing and adoring fans chanting his name.

Olive often wondered if she'd gotten more time with Dad, then maybe she'd have been more like him. More confident, no longer afraid of the spotlight.

"I want my movies to win all the awards. Nickelodeon Kids' Choice, MTV, and the Oscars." Olive's voice grew louder and more assured. "But more than that, I want to make you proud. I wish you were here. Then we could film the Halloween short together. And you could help with my documentary project.

"I guess I'll put my heart and mind into it. Right?"

Olive turned off the recording. Saying her fears out loud had released some of the tightness in her chest.

Olive loved Kayla's ghosts-making-dinner-guests-sing-and-dance idea. Especially as a shout-out to one of her favorite directors. But she couldn't get past having to direct a bunch of people she really didn't know.

What if they make fun of my silent-dinner idea?

What if I freeze?

What if Abigail takes over?

What if she's better than me?

As a future award-winning director, Olive needed to move past the quivering insides. For now, the best she could do was muster up the courage to tell Kayla "Thanks, but no thanks" for her help. She would do it. Tomorrow. Well, she was 20, maybe 10 percent sure she would.

"Just put my heart and mind into it," Olive repeated out loud.

Her thoughts taunted in return, *Yeah, right.*

Chapter Eight

The Big Bad Rodent

THE FOLLOWING EVENING, OLIVE took her time walking toward Kayla's house. The air was crisp and the skies were gray, but luckily it wasn't raining. Bundled in several layers, Olive cinched the hood of her bubble coat tight. With her scarf covering her neck, mouth, and nose, only her fogged-up glasses were visible.

Olive cut across her street and turned right onto the next block. She hiked up her overstuffed backpack. Kayla's and her shared Book of Enchantment took up most of the space, along with all the other required items for a proper sleepover. Like fun-sized bags of Magic M&M's and Sacred Skittles.

Kayla and Olive had started their book of spells in third grade. Their very first spell was a blood oath that they'd stay best friends forever. Neither wanted to actually prick their finger. So instead of blood, Kayla had spat on hers, while Olive had wiped off sweat from her neck. That was four years ago, and they were *still* the best of friends. So obviously magic was real.

Olive stood at the corner and waited for her turn to cross. Once again, she resolved to come clean with Kayla about not needing help with her short. She didn't want to admit that directing Kayla's teammates caused a thought spiral of worst-case scenarios. Instead, she'd tell Kayla about the scene with her dad she'd already had in mind.

After the last vehicle passed, Olive checked both directions before crossing Beaverdale Lane. The dead-end sign to the right caught her attention, and goose bumps shot up her arm.

A fairy-chimes ringtone chirped from her back

pocket. Olive snatched her phone and swiped at the screen. The text from Kayla read: When the teacher asks who is presenting next, followed by a picture of actress Marsai Martin from *Blackish* on *The Daily Show*. Slumped in their chairs, both her and host Trevor Noah appeared to be hiding from the audience.

Olive snorted. She doubted that her biggest inspiration had ever actually shied away from anything. At thirteen, Marsai had become the youngest person ever to produce a movie. Not only had it been her first role in a major Hollywood studio film, but she'd also come up with the idea for the script!

Olive wished she were more like Marsai or Kayla. Her best friend relished performing in front of anyone willing to watch. Dancing since she was five, Kayla had taken ballet, tap, jazz, and even gymnastics. But her favorite dancing style was hip-hop. One of her many dreams was to see her name—KAYLA WATSON—in lights on Broadway. She'd go on and on about the two of them moving to LA, where Olive would film her blockbuster movies and Kayla would win on the show *So You Think You Can Dance.*

The second Olive was about to reply to Kayla's text, someone shrieked, "Stop him!"

Olive's directorial instinct kicked in. She turned on her camera and held up her phone. Her mouth dropped open. An elderly white woman shuffled down the side of the corner house—waving a frying pan!

"That nasty rodent destroyed my property!"

Rodent?

Olive zoomed her camera's view into the overgrown grass, a few steps ahead of the old lady. Her eyes bulged. A large humpbacked animal was awkwardly lumbering for its life! That was no mouse or rat. That was a beaver!

"Waddle?" Olive whispered.

The woman paused and leaned forward, her breathing labored. The pan hung by her side. Her wrinkled face turned back toward the animal with narrowed eyes.

"You won't get away with this!"

With the pan once again raised, the old lady resumed her hunt.

Was anyone else seeing this? Olive swung her head from side to side. Her hood loosened and slid off. She spotted an older kid lugging a large recycling bin to the end of the driveway at the house next door. Their bewildered gaze lingered on the angry old lady. Two adults stood on the front porch of the house across the street. Their animated conversation froze as they stared in horror at the chase.

Olive held her breath. Jumbled thoughts rushed through her head.

I have to do something say something for poor Waddle is it even him or is it some other beaver but does that even matter I should still do something anything but what . . . ?

As the pursuit drew closer, the old woman noticed Olive across the street. She turned her tirade onto Olive.

"Get that camera off me! Doesn't anyone respect privacy anymore? Mind your own business!"

Olive stepped backward, her heartbeat racing. If this old woman was willing to chase a poor helpless beaver, she'd have no problem chasing a twelve-year-old Black girl.

"If you wanna do something, call animal control!" the gray-haired crone spat.

Olive slipped her phone back into her jeans pocket and hustled off toward Kayla's house. The yelling stopped, but she could still hear the woman's shoes stomping through the grass.

Slowing back down to a stroll, Olive thought about Waddle and when they'd first met. She'd initially thought that they'd discovered one of the "rodents at a tremendous size." But instead, it was an enormous, adorable beaver.

Olive came to a halt. *I should do something, right?*

But her anxiety quickly argued, *There* are *other witnesses. What can I really do anyway?*

The teenager would probably tell their parents. They'd call the police or something. And then there was that couple across the street. For sure they would know what to do and take action.

Olive peeked over her shoulder. The older kid and the couple on the porch must have gone back inside. When she turned around, both the crone and the beaver were out of sound and sight.

Chapter Nine

Keep Portland Weird

OLIVE PLOPPED HER HEAVY backpack onto Kayla's unmade bed, trying to forget the awful chase she'd just witnessed. A bulge under the bedspread squirmed. A black cat popped out its head, locked eyes with Olive, then dashed underneath the bed.

"Hello to you too, Twitch," Olive murmured.

The only being Olive had ever known for being more fraidy-cat than herself was Kayla's skittish pet, Twitch. Kayla got the sleek black panther for her sixth birthday over five years ago. He still acted as if he had no idea who Olive was. Or like he didn't want to get too close for fear of who knows what. But Olive couldn't be mad. She understood his timid personality better than anybody. Social situations were a scary thing.

Olive stripped off her bubble coat, scarf, and boots and tossed them onto a pile of clothes littering the rug. Shimmying her shoulders along with a funky song playing, she asked, "Who's this?"

"If you scoop in a whole lot of Zendaya, sprinkle on some Chloe x Halle," Kayla said, rubbing her fingertips together, "and finish off with a dollop of Beyoncé? Then you get Jonáe!"

"Sweet! Like a hot fudge sundae with lots of M&M's."

Kayla made a sour face, definitely because of the added candy topping.

"So, what's the plan for tonight?" Kayla collapsed onto her faux-fur beanbag chair. She picked at her Afro puffs with her fingers. "Makeovers? Movie? There's a new romedy on Friday Flix with that cutie from *Spider-Man*."

Olive wrinkled her nose. Into the latest trends, Kayla

always wanted to try out different hairstyles, outfits, and makeup. She had a ton of makeup because of all the dance performances she did. If she were about to film herself, Olive was all in, otherwise, not so much. And unfortunately, the only movies Kayla ever wanted to watch were cheesy rom-coms.

Ignoring all the options, Olive took out her phone. A lightning of guilt struck her.

"What's wrong?"

Olive exhaled loudly. "You'll never guess what I just filmed."

"Hmm . . ." Kayla furrowed her brows. "A parade of freak bikes, including a tall one for two!

"No wait! A squirrel sitting on a throne eating corn on the cob. When he caught you filming, he threw his half-eaten cob right at your head!"

Olive gave a half smile but couldn't shake Waddle from her thoughts.

The saying "Keep Portland Weird" was no joke. Kayla's suggestions may have sounded ridiculous, but Olive had captured both on film while wandering through their neighborhood. Well, everything except for the squirrel launching corn on the cob at her head. It had kept on eating. But neither girl would've been shocked if that had happened too.

An old lady chasing a beaver was definitely weird. But instead of excitement, Olive felt a heaviness in her chest. She cued up the video and handed Kayla her phone.

Kayla's smile soon faded. She covered her open mouth as the crone's voice growled, "Get that camera off me!"

Once the video ended, Kayla lowered the phone into her lap. "What in the Hansel and Gretel was that?" she muttered in disbelief.

"Right?" Olive nodded. "What was she going to do with that frying pan?"

"Ugh, I don't even want to think about it." Kayla shuddered. "Do you think that was Waddle?"

Olive's stomach fluttered. Yes, and she couldn't stop thinking about it. But she didn't want to believe it.

"Who knows?" Olive shrugged.

Twitch tiptoed out from underneath the bed and settled into Kayla's lap. Kayla stroked his silky fur. "Maybe you should tell somebody."

Olive quickly shook her head. "Nah, there was a

couple across the street who saw it all. It's a grown-up problem for grown-ups to deal with."

Kayla groaned with an exaggerated eye roll. "Seems like all their problems are getting passed down for us to fix."

"Humph." Olive shoved aside a stuffed panda and settled onto Kayla's bed.

"But seriously," Kayla continued, "what if they don't do anything? Imagine if it was Waddle. Or Twitch."

Olive pulled her legs in toward her chest. She couldn't make eye contact. Not with Kayla or Twitch. As his purrs grew louder, her body stiffened.

Olive imagined some of the things she could have done in that moment. Like standing up to that old lady, blocking her path and telling her to back off. If only she'd had a yellow-bladed lightsaber or a magic wand possessed with a manticore's claws. Or maybe she should've called someone. Too bad she didn't have a Bat-Signal to summon a superhero to save the day.

Olive chewed on her thumbnail. She'd done nothing.

Lifting her head, Olive reluctantly stared at Twitch snuggled in Kayla's lap. Stinging warmth spread across her cheeks as if she were being poked with hot needles. It was all too much!

Kayla took over my short. I get lousy teammates. Abigail gets Esme. I have to speak in front of the whole school! Poor Waddle. I wish I'd done something. I want to speak up. But I just can't!

Get in that crone's face? No way! Even with a lightsaber or magic wand, Olive was more like the cowardly lion from *The Wizard of Oz*. Call someone? When she couldn't even bring herself to call Pizza Schmizza?

There *were* other witnesses. She wished Kayla would leave her alone.

"I've decided to do something else for my Rose City film, so the dance team and your choreography won't be needed."

Olive's eyes widened. Those words had just shot out!

"I mean," Olive stumbled, "thanks for offering, but there's this other idea I want to do."

Kayla shrugged. "That's cool." Her voice sounded indifferent. Not as if she didn't care, but rather that she was okay with Olive's decision.

That's it?

Olive had spent two days stressing over the situation! Now that she'd finally said something and gotten what she wanted—no judgy cast to direct—Olive didn't feel any relief. Instead, she was furious. Not at Kayla, but at herself.

"What are you filming instead?" Kayla removed Twitch from her lap and rummaged through the open jewelry box on her dresser.

Olive explained the Halloween-dinner idea with her and her dad, then being ambushed by zombies. With exaggerated hand gestures, she tried to fake enthusiasm. But her self-loathing was eating her up. Why had she wasted all that time avoiding the topic in the first place?

"I love that," Kayla said. "And, of course, I'll play a zombie. I'm sure my brothers will too. They love your films."

She held up a pair of silver hoop earrings to either side of her face, staring at her reflection with pursed lips. "Did you hear about V-Day?"

Olive frowned. "Sounds like some kind of doomsday event."

Kayla laughed. "The school's Valentine's Day dance."

Olive's stomach flipped.

"There's going to be a DJ in the gym, and board games and snacks in the cafeteria."

"Cool," Olive said flatly.

"Don't sound so excited." Kayla made a silly face. "Everyone on the dance team has been talking nonstop about it. Some were thinking we should go as a group. You know, girls *and* boys."

"Oh" was all Olive could manage. This event definitely felt like the end of the world, because she'd never be a part of it.

Josh had said Kayla was a great dancer. Peter had told Kayla she was pretty. No boy had ever said anything like that about Olive before.

One, she was a horrible dancer. But only Kayla knew this fact because Olive had never—and would never—bust a move in public. Two, Olive wasn't pretty. Not like Kayla, anyway. Kayla was beautiful twenty-four seven. Even if she was sweaty and all out of breath after a dance routine. Or when she woke up wearing her silk head wrap. She had beautiful dark skin, striking dark eyes, and the brightest smile.

"Maybe you could go with us? And invite Bobby?" Kayla wiggled her brows.

Olive stuck out her tongue and threw the stuffed panda at Kayla.

"Okay!" Kayla held her hands in front of her face. She closed her jewelry box and settled back into the bean bag chair. "Remember when Abigail mentioned that Cindy was moving away? I've decided to try out for cocaptain of the dance team."

"Cool!" This time Olive said it with real excitement. And not only because she was happy to move on from doomsday dances and boys.

"I think it's time," Kayla said, "to consult the Magic M&M's and Sacred Skittles."

Chapter Ten

The Future Is as Sweet as Candy

OLIVE AND KAYLA'S SPELLS and readings always started the same way, with a pinkie promise. They interlocked their right pinkie fingers and at the same time said, "This is just between us."

Facing one another, they sat cross-legged on the plush rug. A red plate sat in front of Kayla, a blue one in front of Olive. To Olive's right, their Book of Enchantment lay between them, opened to the bookmarked page titled "The Future Is as Sweet as Candy."

Having read their future so many times before, they didn't need to consult their own rules. But it was always part of the routine. A lit cinnamon-scented candle to Olive's left completed the circle. Hovering close to Kayla, Twitch stared at the dancing flame.

Olive handed Kayla one of the fun-sized Skittles bags and took a small bag of the M&M's for herself. She grinned as she thought about how they'd ended up choosing the fortune-telling candies.

When it came to food, Olive and Kayla agreed on mostly everything. No gravy on biscuits. Waffles were best eaten as sandwiches with a peanut butter and marionberry jam spread. And blended boba tea at 50 percent sweet and extra tapioca was far superior to any other drink.

The only thing they disagreed on was candy. Olive's favorite was M&M's and Kayla's was Skittles. It was one of their first big fights way back in third grade, but they'd quickly reconciled once realizing they could exchange their Halloween take. Dressed up as a fortune teller, Olive had joked that there would be lots of candy in their future.

"If only M&M's and Skittles could really tell us what's gonna happen," Kayla had said.

"Maybe they can," Olive had replied. Later that night, they'd added the fortune-telling rules to their book of spells.

Five years later, Olive still loved consulting with the magical candies. "Do you know what you're gonna ask?"

"Looks like Abigail is the only other one trying out for cocaptain," Kayla said, "and I'm super nervous. She's amazing."

"Yeah, but you're awesome too," Olive argued, "and everyone loves you, while Abigail is just . . . you know, Abi."

Kayla's eyes remained heavy with worry. "She's also a strong leader."

"So are you!"

"I don't know," Kayla muttered. She poked at one of her Afro puffs. Twitch bumped his head against her leg, purring.

Though Olive had first learned about magic from movies, it was Kayla's aunt Tabitha, or Aunt T, as everyone called her, who had taught Kayla and Olive all about it.

Her aunt was a witch—and not some wannabe Prudence Blackwood, Bonnie Bennett, or one of the Leopard People from *Akata Witch*. Aunt T was a real-life witch in a real-life coven. Being pagan, she was an expert on magic. There was cool stuff like spells and fortune-telling. But it wasn't about putting curses on others using ingredients like warts from a toad. And it wasn't flying on a broomstick to play sports or make deliveries.

It was the unexplainable, sometimes unimaginable, but undeniable truth. Magic was real.

Sometimes people got so used to the everyday magical stuff that they forgot it's even there. Like when you're feeling blue and suddenly the rain starts to clear, and a rainbow appears. Or when you think about your best friend and they text at that exact moment. That happened with Olive and Kayla a lot. When Kayla had texted earlier that day about spending the night, Olive had replied, Jinx! It was their way of saying, "I was just thinking about you too!"

Kayla gently shook the unopened Skittles bag over her plate. "Will I be the new dance team cocaptain?"

She tore open the bag and a shower of Skittles

clanked onto the dish. They watched the candies bounce and roll around. Once they'd settled into place, Kayla studied the pieces.

Laughing, Kayla stamped her bare feet. Twitch yowled. He wasn't a fan of loud noise.

"Not only are all fifteen *S*s showing," Kayla said, "but there are more strawberry-flavored candies than any other flavor! Woo-hoo!"

"See," Olive said, "you're destined to win. The Sacred Skittles never lie."

"But Abigail's such a force, you know?" Kayla held her palm high above the candle's flickering flame. "Anything's possible, but it won't be easy. I could really use your help."

"Whatever you need," Olive said.

"Abigail and I will each get a turn to lead the team at a home basketball game. Then everyone on the squad, including Abi and me, will get to vote on who we think is best."

"Wonder who Abi will pick." Olive snorted.

"I know school spirit isn't your thing, but it would mean everything if you'd come to my game. I could use a friendly face in the stands."

"Promise." Olive drew an *X* across her chest.

Kayla beamed. "It's your go."

Olive picked up her fun-sized M&M's bag. Clutching it between her palms, she thought about what she wanted to ask. It was important to word it as a "yes, no, or maybe" question, and to be specific. You don't want to say "Will I win?" and then play Candy Crush when you're really asking about a film competition.

The first question that popped into her mind was *Will I get Mr. Dodd's backing for Rose City?* Olive considered other options. *Does Bobby like me? Will I get into film camp?* She shoved away the thought *Was that Waddle being chased?*

She decided to follow her gut.

Olive shook the small brown bag and with total concentration asked, "Will I receive Mr. Dodd's personal recommendation for film camp?"

She tore open the bag, and the M&M's rattled onto her plate. Olive stared intently. She hugged her stomach as two blue-colored pieces—her favorite color—rolled off onto the rug. Twitch sniffed the unfortunate candies.

"Twitch!" Kayla snapped. He dashed to safety underneath the bed.

"Outlook hazy," Olive whispered.

"At least it's not a guaranteed impending doom," Kayla offered.

Olive remained quiet, staring at the two annoying candies.

"That means there's still a chance at success. We could do our 'Make It Come True' spell."

"Nah," Olive said. "Let's watch your rom-com instead."

"You sure? We can watch something else if you want," Kayla said.

"I'm good." Olive wasn't in a movie-watching kind of mood. But she didn't want to talk about all the things wrong in her life anymore either.

"Okay." Kayla picked out all the strawberry Skittles pieces and popped them into her mouth.

As the movie started, Olive stared at the screen, but she didn't pay any attention. Not getting asked to dance by Bobby Filmore, or any other boy, Olive could handle. It's not like she was even any good at dancing. Plus, she'd die if anyone laughed at her moves. But not getting into Rose City? That was her worst nightmare.

Olive knew that her Halloween-dinner short would be good, especially now that she didn't have to direct girls from the dance team. But with the fierce competition and limited spots, she could really use that recommendation.

The "future-is-hazy" prediction had to be because of her teammates, David and Jo. But Kayla was right. There still was a chance at success. Olive's team could still get the highest grade.

Magic was also a verb. It happened when you took action.

Olive just had to push past her comfort zone and lead the team into making the best documentary trailer ever. Like any great director would do. Between Jo's pushy personality and David's blah taste, it wouldn't be easy. But Olive doubted that becoming the world's best fantasy film director would be easy either.

If Marsai Martin, Tim Burton, and Gillian Vansant could make their dreams come true, then so could Olive. Once she figured out how to ignore the fear twisting her belly.

Chapter Eleven

KidVid

OLIVE DESPERATELY WANTED TO change her hazy out-look and receive Mr. Dodd's Rose City seal of approval. She squirmed on the stiff couch. The television was play-ing another one of Dad's favorite childhood movies, *The Goonies.* But Olive's eyes were glued to the screen in her hands. She was looking for inspiration on her favorite app, KidVid.

The documentary project had to be about the school cafeteria. But each team could focus on whatever they wanted, as long as it had something to do with the lunchroom. So the most important step to making the best trailer meant choosing the best documentary focus.

Olive typed "school cafeteria" in the search box. The screen flooded with images. She scrolled through the posts, scanning for anything that sparked ideas.

There were tons of photos of the usual school-served lunches. Stuff like greasy pizzas and oddly colored hamburgers. Some pictures showcased brown-bag lunches. The most interesting was of sushi rolls with a side of seaweed salad. It might be fun to talk about inedible or uncommon school meals. But Olive feared that Jo would push for an in-your-face "Why is it so hard to make decent vegan meals?" exposé.

Not wanting to deal with Jo turning fun into fanatic, Olive kept searching.

She giggled at the silly drawings of doughnuts. She gagged at the suspicious chunks inside cups of green Jell-O. But so far Olive wasn't dazzled with any ideas that would impress Mr. Dodd. With a heavy sigh, she continued to scroll.

Olive paused on a meme of a lunch tray with a

half-eaten pile of mac 'n' cheese. A stock image of Luke Skywalker was superimposed on top, along with the words WHAT DID THE LUNCH LADY SAY TO LUKE SKYWALKER? "USE THE FORKS, LUKE!"

Mr. Dodd was always telling corny jokes. And what filmmaker didn't love *Star Wars*? But Olive didn't know how to turn dad jokes, fantasy films, and the school cafeteria into a documentary. Frustrated, she clicked on the group Fantasy Movies.

Olive loved watching and making fantasy films, so talking about it seemed like a no-brainer. But it didn't matter whether she was with the people she loved most or in film class, Olive often stayed silent.

Sure, she'd give Mom and Kayla updates on some great flick she'd just watched or her latest directorial ideas. They'd both be excited for Olive, but it wasn't the same as talking with people who loved making movies. Kind of like how Olive felt when Kayla was talking about dancing or boys.

Fear of saying the wrong thing had Olive keeping her mouth shut in class. What if everyone thought she was weird? What if they laughed? What if they realized she was a total fraud? And that she'd never be an award-winning fantasy film director?

KidVid, however, was the one space where she could not only lurk and search, but she could also share and engage without falling into a vortex of negative thoughts. Users' identities were completely unknown. You couldn't use your name and any faces in photos and videos had to be hidden. Olive never had to worry about triggering her attention allergy.

Inside the Fantasy Movies group, Olive posted the following: *Middle school documentary project on school cafeteria. Don't want to do the obvious. Ideas?*

As Olive waited for a response, Mom came bustling through the front door. Even though it was a Sunday, Mom was once again working. Hardly a day went by when she wasn't. The only difference was that on weekends she didn't wear a suit.

Mom plopped onto the couch. "I ordered pizza for dinner. Pepperoni, of course. Should be here any minute."

"Cool," Olive said without taking her eyes off her tablet.

Mom switched the channel to the local news. "How was your day today, honey?"

"Okay." Still no comments on her post.

"Finished all your homework?"

"Yup."

"Did all your chores?"

"Uh-huh."

"Completed your quest for world domination?"

Olive let out an amused "Humph" and sat up in her seat when her message notification dinged. Finally!

"Glad to hear your string of one-word answers remains intact."

Olive grinned. "Yep."

Mom's chuckle cut short when the doorbell rang.

"Must be the pizza!" Mom jumped from the couch and hustled to the front door.

Olive read the comments under her post:

Free lunch!
How about giving the cafeteria an
upgrade? Recliners, bumping music,
mood lighting!
Friday local restaurant deliveries!
Food fight!!!

Olive pondered over the suggestions. Food fights could be interesting. Though she'd never actually been in one, she'd seen quite a few in movies. And like every other student—and probably every kid in Portland, Olive *had* heard of the legendary food fight that had happened at Cascadia Middle School way back in ancient history, before people carried around their phones. The Food Fight of 1988.

Olive smiled to herself as a fantastical documentary began to form.

"Here you go!" Mom held out a plate with two large slices.

Olive happily took it.

The news anchor's voice interrupted Olive's attempt at a first bite.

"Earlier today a local resident stumbled upon an awful surprise while taking their usual walk in a southeast Portland neighborhood. A male beaver was found dead near some overgrown hedges. It's unclear if the death was intentional or from natural causes. We've reported in the past the struggle between residents and wildlife getting along. . . ."

Olive put down her slice. That was *her* neighborhood on the screen. She recognized the park less than a mile away. Kayla and her were just there, searching for R.A.A.T.S.

Was it . . . ? Could it be . . . ?

Her jaw clenched.

"Absolutely devastating. I couldn't believe my eyes. I wasn't sure if the beaver was alive or dead, so I called the Oregon Department of Fish and Wildlife and . . ."

The reporter was interviewing the local resident, their face hidden. Even their voice was distorted, the pitch so high, it sounded as if they'd inhaled a helium-filled balloon. Olive wondered if they were one of the other witnesses from yesterday's chase.

She shook her head in disbelief. This was all her fault. Kayla was right. Olive should've done something. She should have told someone about the old lady chasing the beaver. Then maybe Waddle would still be alive.

Chapter Twelve

No Do-Overs

IN HER ROOM, OLIVE ignored her tablet as it dinged again and again. She slumped in her director's chair, her last name emblazoned in white across the black cloth. Real directors commanded instruction and guidance, along with control over the scene. Olive had done none of these things. And now Waddle was dead.

Olive stared at her uneaten pizza. All she'd done was stand on the sidelines, filming the scene. Her stomach churned. She pushed aside her plate.

The worst part was it wasn't just any beaver. It was *Waddle*. Somewhere, there might be a baby beaver that was missing their father.

Olive watched the beaver-chase video. The elderly woman hobbled through the grass, waving a frying pan. Olive's cheeks burned.

"Why didn't I do anything?" she muttered, a thickness in her throat.

The old crone's voice spat, "If you wanna do something, call animal control!"

Olive cringed. Even the old lady had challenged her to do something. But Olive's ridiculous insecurity had insisted that it wasn't necessary. If only she'd paid attention to her gut—instead of her panic—and done something!

Olive watched the chase again. In the middle of her third viewing, she switched it off and randomly hit play on an old video message from Dad.

He was in the backyard, sitting in the shade on a bright summer day. The camera must have been on a tripod, because his entire body was in the shot and he kept fiddling with his hands. Instead of his usual smile, Dad wore a somber look.

"Twenty years ago, my parents died in a car accident," he said. "I was sixteen, and my last word was 'Later.' We never know when it's going to be the last time when we see someone. So I'm grateful I hugged them good-bye. But today I was hit with the memory of my biggest regret. I had bullied a classmate."

Even though it wasn't the first time Olive had watched this, her skin still prickled.

"I was in eighth grade and there was this new scrawny kid. My best friend was a real cool cat. Nobody messed with him. So when he started picking on this kid, calling him names, shoving him in the halls, for no reason . . . I—I said nothing. Sometimes I even laughed and called him names too."

Dad's gaze dropped to his hands twisting his wedding ring. After a long pause, he looked into the camera head-on.

"Eventually, that kid left. Transferred to another school. I have no idea where he is today. I often wonder if he's okay. If he's forgiven me. But I do know that I'm ashamed I didn't do something. I was scared. I didn't want to lose my friend. And I didn't want him to start bullying me.

"There are no do-overs. What's done is done. But we can always own up to our mistakes. We can learn from them and try to do better moving forward."

Even though the video wasn't finished, Olive turned it off. She cleaned her glasses with her shirt and slipped them back on.

If there's one thing Olive knew about magic, it was that it was important to pay attention to the signs. And this video hadn't been chosen by accident.

Life wasn't a fantasy movie. She didn't have a magic clock where she could turn the hands and go back in time and do it all over again. Like Dad had said, what's done is done. But what could she do for poor Waddle now? She couldn't bring him back.

Olive's thoughts wandered to when Kayla and she were in the park. They'd found Waddle instead of R.A.A.T.S. Then to the cemetery, where the Beevers headstone had freaked out Kayla. Two days later, Kayla had texted her right after she'd crossed— Wait!

How did I miss that?

When walking to Kayla's house, Olive had noticed the DEAD END sign when crossing *Beaver*dale Lane. It had made her uneasy in the moment, but she'd totally missed the signs! And then she'd ignored her instincts. Like Dad, Olive had said nothing. Even when she'd seen something happening that hadn't felt right.

The notification on Olive's tablet chimed.

Holding her breath, Olive returned to the KidVid screen. Instead of checking her messages, she uploaded the beaver-chase video. She hid the old lady's face with a wicked-witch sticker. Underneath, she typed, *What would you do if you saw this IRL?* and hit post.

Olive let out a shaky exhale.

She regretted not speaking up for that poor beaver. She'd made a mistake. But she wanted to learn from it. Olive was finally doing something. And magic happened when you took action.

Within minutes, comments filled her screen:

Run

Call 911

Is this for real??

No way. This is fake.

That old lady's ridiculous!

For realsies!

Truth!

Scream

Cry

Tell my parents

Would you really?

What could they do? Even at that

speed, she'd be long gone.

Would they even believe you?

Mine would say "mind your own

business"

Don't be a tattletale

Freak out!

Chase her and see how she likes it

The comments kept coming. Shocked, Olive cleaned her glasses again. She slipped them back on and rapidly blinked. She couldn't believe it.

There were already over a hundred comments! Hardly any of them had said that they would tell anybody about the chase. Most users had posted a string of emojis, usually a face bawling or a face with its head exploding. Or they'd said that they would have saved themselves and gotten out of there quick.

Even more surprising, her video got more likes and shares than she'd ever received on a post! A part of her felt huge relief. Olive wasn't alone in keeping quiet. She logged out of KidVid and lay on her bed. Her phone and tablet remained on her desk. She fidgeted with her hands. Another part of her still weighed heavy with regret.

Olive stared at the ceiling. She wanted to message her father about everything that had happened. But what she wanted more than that was for him to say that she wasn't a horrible person and that everything would be okay.

It didn't seem to matter whether she took action or remained silent. The tug-of-war between relief and regret never seemed to end.

Chapter Thirteen

Tug-of-War

OLIVE COULDN'T BELIEVE THE Monday she was having.

Every time she checked her beaver chase post on KidVid, the likes, shares, and comments had increased. There were almost five hundred likes! But it didn't end there.

She'd gotten an A on her science test, and in Spanish class, Bobby Filmore had smiled at her! Well, maybe it was more like a quick nod in her direction. But Kayla had witnessed the entire thing—along with squealing about it after class—so Olive knew that something had happened.

More and more, relief was winning against regret in the tug-of-war!

As Olive neared the room for film class, there was a skip to her step. During breakfast, she'd practiced her food-fight pitch. With this documentary focus, they were sure to get the Rose City recommendation!

"Happy Monday, Olive," Mr. Dodd said.

"Hello." She waved, her usual hurried gait now an upbeat mosey. She eyed his frog-print bow tie and matching suspenders. "Cool frogs, Mr. Dodd."

"So glad it makes you *hoppy*!" He chuckled. "Don't forget, for the next month everyone will be sitting with their teams."

Olive spotted the empty seat by David and Jo in the back corner of the room. Sure, they weren't the teammates she'd hoped for, but that didn't matter. Successful directors thrived under pressure. Surely her idol Marsai Martin didn't complain when she had to work with people not at the top of her list. Marsai would make it work. And so would Olive.

Control, Olive Blackwood. Must learn control.

"This is going to be so much fun!" David leaned forward as she settled into her chair. "Don't you think?"

"Tons," Olive said, pushing up her red glasses.

Jo cocked an eyebrow, giving Olive a once-over look. A slight chill ran through Olive.

Before Jo had a chance to say anything, the bell rang and Mr. Dodd started class.

"If two vegans get in a fight," he said, "is it still considered a beef?"

Groans echoed throughout the room. Jo doubled over with snort-laughter.

Mr. Dodd grinned. "As you know, we're making documentary trailers about the school cafeteria. And each team will also write up a detailed plan. This will include footage, storytelling techniques, and information resources you would've liked to have used if you were making the full documentary.

"Today you'll begin brainstorming to pick your team's name and focus for this topic." Hands clasped, he glided back and forth in front of the class. "Remember, you must get my approval for your topic and initial plan by the end of the week. But first let's wrap up our conversation about the trailers and clips we watched on Friday.

"We started discussing different storytelling techniques. Can anyone remind the class of some examples?"

Mr. Dodd leaned against his desk. Hands shot up into the air.

"Abigail?" he called, even though her hand wasn't up.

"Interviews," she said, flipping her hair.

Mr. Dodd nodded. "With whom?"

"Most were with the film's subject, like those unhoused kids here in Portland."

"Who else was interviewed?" Mr. Dodd asked. "Esme?"

"Experts. There were scientists in the global warming one."

"And with the senator who didn't believe in climate change," Jo added.

"Correct. The opposition," Mr. Dodd said. "What are some other storytelling techniques we saw? Olive?"

Olive rubbed the back of her neck. Her knee bounced uncontrollably, but she managed to squeak out, "Um, reenactments? When the one unhoused kid stole the other kid's stuff."

Mr. Dodd smiled warmly. "Nice. Anyone else?"

"All of them had a narrator."

"Stock footage of the Black Lives Matter march."

"Very good, class." Mr. Dodd clapped. "Now let's get busy brainstorming!"

Chairs scraped along the linoleum floor as students rearranged their seats. Many conversations exploded at once. Olive faced her teammates head-on as Jo began to share the ideas they and David had already come up with.

"The first thing anyone thinks about when you say cafeteria is food," said Jo. "Doesn't matter if the food is gross or delicious, because it's a tragedy if everyone's needs aren't met.

"I can't imagine life without bread, but my cousin has celiac disease, so she can't have gluten." Hands clamped on their desk, Jo leaned in. "That means no pizza, no hamburger or hot dog buns, and no rolls. And don't even get me started about the lack of vegan options."

Olive's mood soured as she recalled Jo's outburst at the lunch lady last week. But she nodded along, trying to keep a happy face.

"Or we could talk about our meals' nutritional values and whether we're getting something from all the food groups." Jo continued to take up space, their waving arms spread wide.

Olive kept bouncing her head up and down, but she wasn't feeling any of their ideas. Their group needed a focus that would get students excited since they'd be voting for their favorite trailer at the evening assembly.

She eyed Mr. Dodd wandering around the room. He paused at Esme and Abigail's team.

They also needed to impress their teacher since he had the final say on their grade. Something fun and unique, but with an educational slant. Her food-fight idea would be perfect.

"Or we could ask about food inspections," David added. "When were they? Did they pass? You know, focus on food safety and management."

Olive wrinkled her nose. She thought about suggesting taking samples to see how much poop and dead insects they could find to up the wow factor. But it still didn't seem enough on such a snooze of a topic.

"But . . . don't you think pretty much everyone will focus on food?" Olive said timidly.

"Well, duh." Jo made a face. "I just said it's the first thing that comes to mind, but how many teams will talk about dietary needs?

"Did you know that at least two students per classroom will have a food-allergy reaction? Between milk, eggs, and peanuts, it's no surprise. But what's being done to prevent it?"

Olive was sinking in her seat under Jo's booming voice. She silently repeated her favorite word to calm her nerves: *Control. Control. Control.*

"We could always ask students how they feel about the lunchroom," David suggested. "What they like and what they don't. That way it's not only about food, but also about the service and the cafeteria itself."

"Yeah." Jo's head bobbed up and down. "We could make an app for all the students and teachers to review. They could rate each category, from one to five stars, and leave comments."

"Sounds like a lot of work," Olive said. "With having to make a trailer and write up a plan."

Jo frowned. "For someone with a lot of opinions, you're not making any suggestions."

Olive's cheeks stung. She clamped her lips shut, afraid to go against Jo. Her good mood had dissolved into misery.

"How about we come up with a team name instead?" David said. "Any suggestions?"

"Nope." Jo looked at Olive, as if challenging her to say something.

Olive fidgeted in her chair.

Jo folded their arms tight across their chest.

Olive's sour mood grew rancid.

"How are we doing over here?" Mr. Dodd said cheerily, tugging on his suspenders.

"Not. Great." Jo huffed.

Olive's eyes widened. She agreed with Jo, but she never would've said that to a teacher.

"We can't agree on anything." Jo gave Olive a glare. "We can't even come up with a team name!"

"That's okay." Mr. Dodd flashed a sympathetic smile.

"Keep talking it out. I'm confident you'll come up with something great."

He glanced at the wall clock. "Class is almost over, so just sleep on it tonight and start fresh tomorrow. Even though your initial plan only needs a brief description and a list of ideas, you'll want to pick a focus by tomorrow. Because how can you map out a plan if you don't know your destination?"

The second the final bell rang, Jo jumped from their seat and stormed out of the classroom.

Olive exchanged a wary look with David.

"No biggie," he said. "We'll figure it out tomorrow."

Olive released a heavy sigh. She wasn't so sure.

Chapter Fourteen

Food Fight!

OLIVE'S STELLAR MONDAY HAD turned into a huge flop.

She'd chickened out in sharing her food-fight idea with David and Jo. Kayla had dance practice after school, so Olive rode the bus home alone. And no matter how many times she silently said *Must learn control,* she couldn't shake the negative chatter swirling in her head.

Mom, of course, was working late. So Olive sat alone watching *Ghostbusters: Afterlife* while poking at leftover meatloaf with her fork. Then just as she was about to text Kayla, she discovered that her phone *and* tablet were dead. Once again, she'd forgotten to charge them.

The next day at lunch, Abigail sauntered up to Kayla and Olive's table.

"Ohmygosh," she said, her gaze heavy on Olive. "Aren't you *so* excited about our documentary trailer? Our team has the best topic *ever*."

Abigail rambled on about how they were focusing on the different lunchroom cliques. Where they hung out, what they ate, blah, blah, bleh.

Kayla gave Olive a slight shrug and then changed the conversation to the dance team.

When Abigail finally left, Olive caught Kayla up on yesterday's no-named-team fiasco.

"Ugh," Kayla huffed. "Mean Vegan Jo better not ruin your project."

She appreciated her best friend's support. But for the first time, Olive dreaded going to film class.

Olive resumed her hurried gait past Mr. Dodd's cheery "Welcome, Olive!" and gave him a small wave.

The M&M's were clear about my hazy future.

Olive sank into the desk next to David.

It's up to me to fix this. Dad said I can do anything I put my mind to.

Unfortunately, Olive had -30 percent confidence in this statement.

Jo stomped into class and plopped into their seat next to Olive. Their scowl sent shivers down Olive's spine. She hung her head, swallowing hard.

"Okay, class," Mr. Dodd said. "Let's keep on brainstorming! I'll walk around and check in with everyone, but feel free to ask any questions."

"How about," David said slowly, "we focus on all the people who make our lunch possible? Students often forget everything that cafeteria workers do."

Jo folded their arms. "Well, it's not about food so someone should be happy."

Olive's face grew hot, her nerves stretching into irritation.

"Um." David looked back and forth between Olive and Jo. "You know how Mr. Dodd taught us word-association brainstorming in English last year?"

They both nodded.

"Good. You'll each take turns calling out a word that pops into your head until we find an idea everyone agrees on," David said. "Jo, why don't you go first?"

"Food," Jo said.

Olive's jaw clenched. "Stinks."

"Cheesy." Jo narrowed their eyes.

"Salty."

"Sweet." Jo smirked.

"M&M's."

"Junk."

"Fight!" Olive cried. "*Food* fight!"

"I thought you didn't want to focus on food." Jo rolled their eyes. "And the only suggestion you can come up with is food fight? Wow. Original."

"Not just any food fight," Olive said. "The Food Fight of 1988."

David's eyes widened. Jo held a pinched expression.

There was no telling how many versions of the food-fight legend existed. Maybe one for every school year since Cascadia Middle School opened in 1912. The underlying plot was always the same, but key details always changed. Olive had heard three different accounts, and shared each of them with David and Jo.

Olive and Kayla had first learned about the accidental food fight when they were little. They'd overheard Kayla's oldest brother telling her second oldest brother the day before he'd started middle school. The legend had gone like this:

Redheaded Fred was crushing on this girl named Lizzy but was too afraid to talk to her. So one day he mustered the courage to let her know in his own unique way. On pink construction paper with a black Sharpie, he wrote: *Will you BEE my Valentine?* along with a doodle of a buzzing bee. He folded the note into a paper airplane and during lunch threw it in her direction. Freaked out by the speeding UFO, some other student dropped their soda. They spilled it on their neighbor and someone yelled, "Food fight!" An apple hit poor redheaded Fred in the head and he fell into a coma. Embarrassed, Lizzy moved far away. Fred never woke up, and to this day, students may catch Fred's ghost weeping in the cafeteria.

When Olive and Kayla were in third grade, Kayla's

twin brothers had told them a different version. Instead of shooting a paper airplane, Fred had held up a sign that said: *Will you be my Valentine?* Earlier, he'd released all the frogs from the science lab into the lunchroom. All because he'd known that Lizzy loved animals.

One of the frogs had jumped onto a student's lap. They'd accidentally tossed their mashed potatoes, starting the most infamous—and only—food fight in Cascadia Middle School's history. Just like the other tale, Fred had fallen into a coma. But this time, students might hear the ghosts of the lab frogs ribbit in the lunchroom.

Finally, at the start of Olive and Kayla's sixth-grade year, rumors about the Food Fight of 1988 had spread. This time—because Lizzy loved music—Fred had had the eighth-grade choir sing the chorus from "Girl You Know It's True." One of the singers sneezed on a student's sandwich. Grossed out, the student had chucked their lunch. It landed on someone else, once again turning into a food fight! One might even catch the ghosts of the choir humming that popular eighties tune.

The silence from Olive's teammates was deafening.

Did I say too much? Did I speak too fast? Did I get too carried away?

Ugh, my future is still hazy.

Jo's face softened. Their downward brows straightened out as a smile appeared. "I like it."

Olive's jaw dropped.

"It's got everything!" Jo bubbled with excitement. "Drama, fantasy, fact, rumors. We can do reenactments, interviews, the works!"

"I have the perfect name for our team." David beamed. "What's Up, Doc!"

Olive and Jo stared at each other.

At the same time, they both grinned, turned to David, and said, "Yes!"

Chapter Fifteen

It's Okay To "Take"

THE REST OF FILM class zoomed by. When the final bell rang announcing the end of the school day, Olive whipped out her phone. Her KidVid post was up to almost two thousand likes!

"Is that a beaver?" David asked.

Olive startled. Most students had already left the room. She hadn't expected David and Jo to be standing there, staring with questioning eyes.

Olive hesitated, her gaze lingering on the cover

image of her post. A close-up of Waddle.

"Um . . . yeah," she stammered.

"Did you know that beavers can't burp?" said David. "But, man, they sure can pass gas!"

Olive and Jo exchanged surprised looks.

"Many people don't even know that they're rodents. But rodents are the 'beasts that gnaw,' and we all know about beavers and trees. They're the largest member of the rodent family in North America!"

Olive's jaw dropped. So that's why Kayla's brothers had called them R.A.A.T.S.!

"These amazing furry architects and engineers do so much for the environment," David continued. "Their dams are the water recycling system of the world, and they can even stop forest fires. They're also vegetarians!" He wiggled his brows at Jo.

Jo chuckled. "Cool."

David rambled on, sharing a bunch of beaver facts about why they could help save the planet. He was so excited and talking so fast, Olive could barely catch everything he said.

"How do you know all this stuff about beavers?" Olive asked.

"I know *everything* about them!" David gushed. "Both my parents went to Oregon State and are huge Beavers fans. I've been wearing OSU clothes since before I could walk and had pennants and posters on my wall before I could read. It's no surprise I love them with Benny Beaver as their mascot.

"One day I hope to be Benny when I go to OSU. I literally flipped when I made mascot this year!" David beamed.

"Wait," Olive said. "*You're* Leevitt the Beaver?"

Even though Olive had never gone to a school game, she'd been forced to attend pep rallies. And there was that time the cheerleading squad had had an impromptu "rah-rah" session during lunch with Leevitt adding his rambunctious and hilarious flair.

Olive would have never suspected ho-hum David to be the school mascot that everyone loved.

There were school T-shirts with a cartoon beaver on the front that students wore on game days. Even Olive had one. Only because the beaver was adorable and it came in her favorite tan, beige, and muted orange colors. The kind of colors that didn't draw any attention.

"Wow," Olive said, her eyes wide. "That's pretty neat."

"Yeah, it's the best." His face flushed. "Can we see the video?"

Olive's cheeks burned. "Um, yeah, sure." She hit play.

No matter how many times she'd watched it, Olive still cringed when the lady cried "If you wanna do something, call animal control!"

When the video ended, Olive lowered her phone. The silent tension was thick.

"Where did you get that?" David's voice was low and shaky.

Staring at her sneakers, Olive swallowed hard. "I, um, filmed it.

"And, um, the next day I saw an awful news report about a dead beaver in my neighborhood. I'm not sure, but . . ."

Olive's eyes met David's sad gaze. "I wonder if it's the same beaver."

I wonder if it was Waddle.

"You should call the Department of Fish and Wildlife and report the chase," David said. "Maybe they can do something."

Olive's grip tightened around her phone. She didn't want to call. This was so much worse than ordering pizza. Especially with an audience.

Posting the video and getting tons of positive attention may have made Olive feel better. But now she realized that it hadn't changed anything. Maybe if she called, they could determine if it were the same beaver from the news and then hold the old crone accountable. Her heartbeat thudded in her ears.

"Yeah," Jo said, punching their fist into their open palm, "make that old lady pay. Maybe she'll go to jail!"

Olive googled the phone number, then hesitated. She couldn't do it.

It was like the time she couldn't finish her speech. The terror was too much. Olive wished she could make a simple phone call. She wanted so badly to be normal. But she couldn't even get fight or flight right. Instead, she froze.

"What are you waiting for?" Jo asked. "Call!"

Olive locked eyes with David. For a moment, she didn't feel so alone. It seemed like he recognized and understood her fear.

"How about we call them together?" David suggested.

Olive nodded, her jittery nerves melting a little. She hit the call button and put it on speaker.

"Good afternoon," a cheery voice said. "Oregon Department of Fish and Wildlife. How may I help you?"

"Um . . . hi," Olive stammered. "We . . . uh . . . I—"

"We're calling about the dead beaver found in Portland the other day," Jo said, rolling their eyes at Olive.

"And we have a video where some old lady's chasing a beaver," David added.

"Not sure it's the same beaver," Olive's voice squeaked, her heart pounding, "but maybe you could, you know, look into it."

"And do something about it," Jo barked.

There was an uncomfortable pause. Finally, the voice on the other end said, "Oh my, well, that's . . . interesting. Thanks for letting us know. You can send us the video, and we'll look into it, but please know that it's legal to take beavers."

David gasped.

Olive furrowed her brow.

"Take? You mean, like, kidnap?" Jo said.

David's face crumbled as he shook his head no. He drew his finger across his neck and hung his head to one side, his eyes closed and tongue hanging out.

"You mean exterminate?" Jo shrieked.

The voice on the phone coughed. "It's legal for residents to lethally remove beavers when they're causing damage. Beavers are defined as a predatory animal on private land and considered destructive. So, yes, 'take' means to kill, attempt to kill, or obtain possession or control of any wildlife."

Olive's eyes watered.

"Is there anything else I can help you with today?" the voice asked.

"Destructive?" Jo went off, their pale skin growing redder by the second. "Who came up with this absurd—"

"No thank you," Olive hastily said, and hit end.

Chapter Sixteen

Don't Make It Right

"ALL GOOD BACK THERE?" Jo's dad said over the talk news playing on the car radio. He twisted around in the driver's seat and gave Olive a warm smile.

Olive nodded, though she was far from good. "Yes, thanks, Mr. Willems."

"Call me Mo," he said.

Making that call to the Fish and Wildlife people, Olive had lost track of time and missed her bus home. She'd been shocked when Jo had offered her a ride.

They might have gone along with her food-fight project idea, but Olive was certain that Jo didn't like her.

Olive's forehead rested against the car window as they pulled out of the school parking lot. She felt as heavy as the pouring rain with her thoughts not letting up.

It's legal for residents to lethally remove beavers.

To kill or attempt to kill.

Exterminate.

Does that mean it wouldn't have made a difference if I'd said something right away?

Olive hugged her belly. That thought didn't make her feel better. All this new information was making her feel a hundred times worse.

Waddle, a predatory animal? He's a vegetarian! Why would anyone want to "take" him?

To kill or attempt to kill.

Exterminate.

Jo turned down the radio. "Dad, did you know that it's okay to murder beavers?"

Olive caught Mo's eyes widen in the rearview mirror.

"If you mean 'take,' then, sadly, yes," he said.

"It just doesn't seem right." Jo looked over their shoulder to catch Olive's gaze.

Olive's arms tingled. It was pretty cool that Jo supported her.

"Especially if David's right," Jo said. "If they're able to save the planet and all. We should do something about it!"

"But what?" Olive shrugged. "It's . . . the law."

Jo turned back around. "Humph! Don't make it right."

"You know," Mo said, "I volunteered with Busy Beavers years ago. They're a great nonprofit, doing whatever they can, like petitions and protests, to help save the beavers. We should look to see if they still have volunteer meetings."

"That sounds great!" Jo said.

"If you want," Mo said, "I'd be happy to take you and your friend."

Petitions?

Olive tensed. She didn't want to go around asking for signatures like those annoying college students carrying clipboards and blocking the entrance to Trader Joe's.

They always made Mom mad, even if she agreed with their cause.

"Save the Orcas. Combat Climate Change. Register to Vote," Mom would always mutter. "Can't a person just pick up some groceries without getting all political about it?"

Protests? Being vocal? Out loud and in public? In front of strangers?

Olive grew stiff.

"Thanks, Dad," Jo said. "I bet our teammate Leevitt the Beaver would love to go too."

"That's great— Wait, their name is *what*?" Mo said.

Jo burst into laughter.

Olive forced a chuckle, but she didn't say anything.

With their rocky start, Olive didn't want to speak out against a sort of friendlier version of Jo. Getting along with Jo was crucial to doing great on their project and winning the Rose City recommendation.

Plus, there's no way Jo would understand why Olive was afraid of pretty much anything that involved being surrounded by people—especially strangers. Honestly, Olive didn't get it herself. At least Kayla got nervous like a normal person, so she kind of understood Olive's jittery nerves. Jo on the other hand? They weren't afraid of *anything*.

If only Olive hadn't checked her KidVid post in front of David and Jo. Then maybe she wouldn't be in this volunteer mess.

Chapter Seventeen

Leave IT to Beavers

SPENT FROM THE DAY'S events, Olive crashed onto her bed.

She needed to do something to help beavers, but not if it involved talking to or marching with strangers. A sudden ping on Olive's phone startled her from her thoughts. She glanced at her screen. It was Kayla: Where are you?

Olive: Missed the bus.

Hitched a ride with Jo!

Kayla: Mean Vegan Jo???

Olive: I know, right?!

Kayla: Gotta go. Heather & April from dance team are here.

To help with extra practices.

Olive: Break a leg!

Kayla: Ew. NO!

That's for actors. NOT dancers!

Olive: Oops, sorry.

Good luck with hip-hopping?

Smash that shimmy?

Kayla: LOL

SMH

I'm going now.

Olive slid off her bed and wandered into the kitchen. Mom had texted earlier that she'd be at the office late and to have dinner without her.

She shoved a bowlful of leftover spaghetti and meatballs into the microwave. As the microwaved hummed, Olive kept thinking about the ride home. Jo was right. Just because it was legal to exterminate beavers didn't make it okay. Olive had already been silent once, and now Waddle was dead.

After the buzzer sounded, Olive took her dinner back to her room and settled at her desk.

Spinning her fork inside her bowl, Olive thought about all the beaver facts David had recited by heart. The ones she could remember, anyway. Like that they can remain underwater for fifteen minutes or that their large front teeth—the orange ones—never stopped growing! He'd babbled so much info that it had been impossible to keep up.

Olive searched "the benefits of beavers" on her tablet.

A ton of links flooded the screen. She clicked on the first one and shoved a forkful of noodles into her mouth. It was all about climate change and its scary impact in the western US.

Olive didn't want to think about it. Especially after those frightening wildfires two years ago.

Mom and her recycled, composted, and drank water from the tap. Mom used a thermos whenever she treated herself to Stumptown coffee. She even paid for a recycling service to pick up items donation centers wouldn't take, like dead batteries and worn, old clothing. But would any of that really help?

With all the other nerve-racking chatter in her head,

why would Olive want to add global warming to the list? Like how intense and larger wildfires were projected to increase in the West—including Oregon—because of climate change caused by humans.

As Olive continued reading, her eyes widened. She had no idea what a difference beavers made. With every tree that they fell, every dam that they made, and every drop of water stored in their pond, beavers changed the ecology of forests, or even deserts!

These new homes get turned into wetlands, like ponds, marshes, or swamps. Many of the plants and animals that live in them are endangered. These ecosystems, and everyone in it that calls it home, were kept healthy and happy thanks to beavers! And why R.A.A.T.S. wore the title "keystone species."

That's why David had called them furry engineers!

Once she finished reading, Olive returned to the search results and moved on to the next link. This one was about beavers being displaced and people rescuing the unwanted rodents to help find them a new home. She stabbed a meatball with her fork. The more she learned, the angrier she got.

Pretty much everything they did helped the planet. Beavers created homes for fish, mammals, waterfowl, songbirds, amphibians, *and* insects. Their ponds helped prevent floods and droughts. And their lodges even welcomed outside guests to crash during winter. They saved and protected water and animals—including humans.

Olive hesitated on the National Parks website, her gaze lingering on a family of beavers swimming together. Not only were they saving the planet, but their social lives revolved around family.

The mother and father stayed together for life and had one litter a year, with one to four kits. Their young stayed with their parents for about three years, so there could be up to three generations in the lodge—with as many as six to twelve beavers! When a yearling left home, they found their mate and started their own family. Sounded a lot like Kayla's massive clan.

Olive's jaw clenched. Kits were usually found with their dad. Fathers taught their young how to fell trees and help with dam and lodge repairs.

What would life be like if Dad had been around to teach me stuff?

Feeling a pang of jealousy, Olive closed the website.

The only family she had was her mom. And when Mom wasn't working, she was always exhausted. Neither of her parents had any siblings, and she'd never met any of her grandparents.

Restless, Olive chewed on her fingernail. Dad's parents had died in a car crash before she was born. Mom wasn't close with her parents and never talked about why. The only reason Olive knew that they even existed was because they'd send her signed birthday and Christmas cards every year, both with checks for fifty dollars. No note. No return address. Just the signature. Olive wasn't even sure if they'd ever sent Mom anything.

Olive shuddered. What if Waddle had left behind a family? Maybe there was a mother beaver and their yearling wondering where Waddle had gone. Maybe the yearling even had kit siblings.

Pushing away her jittery mood, Olive decided to reach out to the one family member she knew best and who always had time for her. She hit the record button.

"Dad," she said softly. "Remember when I was freaking out about my documentary-project teammates?

Well, I think it's going to work out. Not only did they like my idea on the Food Fight of 1988, but I think we're going to help save beavers.

"Did you know that it's legal to kill them in Oregon? The state animal? Pretty wicked, right? And, well, you know me and making movies, so that's what I'm going to do. I'm going to make short videos to share on KidVid about all the awesome stuff beavers do because if people know the truth, then maybe, I don't know. . . .

"Then maybe things could change. I'm no Greta Thunberg, but I have a voice too."

Olive snorted. Leave it to beavers to finally make her want to speak up. Even if it was from behind a camera.

Chapter Eighteen

Did You Know . . . ?

"DID YOU KNOW BEAVERS make brown goo from a gland near their butt?" Olive said.

She sat at the kitchen island eating Lucky Charms while Mom was making one of her ridiculously large vanilla lattes.

Mom made a disgusted face.

With a touch of a button, Mom's fancy silver machine hissed as milk filled more than half her cup. The grinder whirred, crushing espresso beans. After a few seconds, coffee flowed, turning the milk into a creamy beige.

"It's used to mark their territory, but some weirdos have used this smelly beaver oil not only in perfumes, but in vanilla flavoring." Olive swirled the colorful marshmallows and frosted oats around in her bowl. "Just like the syrup you put into your latte!"

"Seriously, Olive?" Mom set down her glass with an irritated grunt.

"I mean, just because it has a musky, vanilla scent, why would someone think, 'I wanna wear or eat this brown goo'? Gross, right?" Olive continued munching on her cereal.

"What's gotten into you?" Mom asked.

Olive thought about poor Waddle and the Oregon law that said exterminating beavers was okay and all the beaver facts she'd learned yesterday. Especially those facts that proved how beavers helped heal the planet.

"Remember those scary wildfires two years ago?" Olive shuddered. "It got so bad, we could barely see anything outside and it hurt to breathe."

Mom nodded and resumed drinking her latte.

"Beaver restoration is one of the most important things we can do to stop hurting the planet. If we don't do something, the wildfires are gonna get worse." Making fists in her lap, Olive resisted the urge to chew on her nails. "So saving beavers can help reduce them."

"Oh, honey." Mom wrapped her arms around Olive. "I didn't realize how much it still bothered you. Do you want to talk about it?"

Olive shook her head. "I wanna do something about it."

"That's great, sweetie. I'd love to hear more"—Mom glanced at her watch—"but I'm running late. Maybe we can do something about it together."

Olive gave a small smile. She knew her mom meant what she'd said. But she also understood that Mom's work schedule never gave her enough time to do much of anything. Olive, however, was aware of one person who would be as excited as she was with her KidVid plan.

Olive rushed to first period, something she'd never done before because she hated math. Seemed pointless when computers could pretty much calculate everything. But today Olive couldn't get there fast enough.

She hustled into the classroom. It was empty except for David sitting at their shared desk. Not even Ms. White was there yet.

Olive planted her palms onto the desktop. "I've got news!"

David startled, then grinned.

She slid into her chair and turned to David with raised brows. "After all that neat stuff you told us about beavers and that awful call to the Fish and Wildlife people yesterday, I got to thinking, if beavers can do so much to help the planet, then why not help beavers?"

David drummed his feet excitedly against the floor. "What did you have in mind?"

Slowly kids shuffled into the room as the start of class grew closer. Olive hesitated. It was one thing to say it while filming a message to her father. It was another to say it out loud to a live audience.

Olive leaned in, pushed up her glasses, and nervously blurted out, "I wanna make videos about the awesome stuff beavers do and post them on KidVid, and maybe somehow we can do something about that ugly extermination law."

Before David could respond, Marcus and Aiyed stomped into the room.

"Dude, you think you're so acute," Marcus boomed. He shoved Aiyed playfully.

Aiyed strutted to his desk and said, "You know I am from every angle!"

The class burst out laughing.

Ms. White breezed in just as the tardy bell clanged. "So glad to hear that everyone's happy to be in math class today." She shut the door behind her.

Olive slumped in her seat. She was itching to know David's thoughts about her plan. Now she was stuck learning about probability for forty-five minutes.

Ms. White droned on, writing on the whiteboard. A problem about a guy rolling a die and flipping a coin and what was the probability that he'd roll a three and the coin would land heads up.

Olive hung her head. The probability of dying of boredom was 100 percent.

A poke in her shoulder shook Olive out of her

thoughts. She looked at David and then down at the paper he was sliding toward her: *Love it! I have lots of ideas. Let's talk during lunch.*

Olive met David's gaze and gave him a thumbs-up!

The noise of shrieking kids filled the lunchroom, along with the smashed-up smells of bleach, dirty socks, and beef burritos. Olive tore open a packet and dribbled watery chipotle sauce onto her opened tortilla.

"Did you know that the pond in our neighborhood wouldn't exist if it weren't for beavers? And without this pond, the plants and animals that live there would be homeless?

"And that beavers change the ecology of forests? Just by living their everyday normal lives. And to think that we almost trapped them out of existence for some ugly fur hats!"

"Wow," Kayla said, rolling her eyes.

Olive folded her burrito back up and took a bite. She wondered why adults hadn't learned from the first time beavers had almost gone extinct.

"Did I tell you about the V-Day invites?" Kayla asked.

Olive's stomach did a flip. She set her burrito back down.

Next month, the Saturday after her documentary presentation, was the Valentine's Day dance. Unlike other school dances where most students went with a friend or two, this one had everyone talking about who was going with which group. And who thought who was cute and who they were hoping to dance with.

Olive shook her head no.

"All the eighth graders on the dance team are sending a valentine to ask someone to join their group to the dance," Kayla said. "Heather, April, Abigail, and I are talking about starting our own. You should join us. And send a valentine invite to Bobby." Kayla winked.

Olive frowned. "Can I sign it as 'Your Secret Admirer'?"

Kayla made a face. "That kinda defeats the purpose."

"Who are you asking?"

"I was thinking Jeff Miller."

"The guy on the basketball team? Isn't he an eighth grader?"

Kayla shrugged. "What's the worst that could happen?"

Olive could come up with one hundred horrible possibilities. He could laugh in Kayla's face—in front of the entire basketball team—and say, "No way."

Or he could crumple up her valentine and slam-dunk it into one of the large cafeteria trash bins. He could even post the card online, along with an animated basketball pointing at it and laughing, with the header "Nope!"

Those scenarios, however, would never happen to Kayla. Those were the kind of things Olive worried about happening to herself.

"If he says no, then I'll ask someone else," Kayla said matter-of-factly.

Olive wished she could face the world like Kayla, not caring about the outcome. Instead, she found herself drowning in fear, often all the ridiculous reasons pushing her further under.

Control. Must learn control.

Shaking it off, Olive decided to forget about the silly dance. She'd put her attention back onto making reels about beaver facts, and hopefully save beavers like Waddle.

"Did you know that the earliest modern beaver fossil

in North America was found right here in Oregon, and it's seven million years old?" Olive held up her palm, signaling Kayla to let her finish. "And can you believe there used to be giant beavers the size of a black bear? The original R.A.A.T.S.!"

"What have I done to deserve this torture," Kayla teased with a grin.

Before Olive could share the weird stuff humans do with the brown beaver goo, David approached their table.

"Hey." He gave a small wave.

"Perfect timing," Olive said. "I was just schooling Kayla on why beavers are so awesome."

"Save yourself, David." Kayla laughed. "Run while you still can."

"Who do you think first introduced me to beaver facts?" Olive smirked.

"Not you too!" Kayla said.

David blushed. "Yup, I've got all the facts."

Kayla shook her head. "I'd have figured it was Mean Vegan Jo that started all this."

Olive suppressed a giggle.

"That's not nice." David frowned. "Calling them that."

His eyebrows drew close together as he turned toward Olive. "You're okay with calling people names?"

"I mean, they're not really nice, so . . ." Olive shrugged.

"They did just give you a ride home so you didn't have to walk in the rain," David said.

Olive's cheeks burned.

"I thought you were cool." David sighed.

"It's a silly nickname," Kayla said. "We're not hurting anyone."

"Would you say it to Jo's face?" David challenged.

Olive slumped, unable to meet his gaze.

"That's what I thought," David said flatly and walked away.

Chapter Nineteen

In a Perfect World

NAUSEA PUNCHED OLIVE IN the gut and kept on whaling.

"David's overreacting." Kayla shut her locker. "I mean, Jo's been pretty rude to you. I only called them that to lighten the mood."

Olive said nothing.

Even if Jo was loud and opinionated and didn't like Olive, none of that mattered. David was right. She would never call Jo "Mean Vegan Jo" to their face.

Olive pretty much said nothing the rest of the day.

David had avoided her in gym class, and she'd watched the slow-ticking clock all through English, dreading final period.

Hiking up her heavy backpack, Olive trudged through the hallway. She made no effort to avoid the steady stream of students pushing past in both directions.

Will David tell Jo?

If Jo didn't like me before . . .

Maybe David or Jo or both will ask Mr. Dodd to kick me off the team.

The Magic M&M's were right.

I'll never get Mr. Dodd's backing I'll never get into Rose City I'll never be an award-winning director I ruin everything I ruin everything I ruin everything. . . .

Sweaty and shivering, Olive had a sudden urge to get to the bathroom—and quick! Thankfully, it was empty. But she felt no relief, even after her diarrhea attack. She washed her hands, took several deep breaths, and splashed cold water onto her face.

Staring at her reflection, her thoughts once again sounded alarms.

Ugh, how gross!

That hasn't happened since last year.

When I'd frozen during my class speech.

Why now?

Why me?

Maybe I should go see the nurse.

Then I won't have to face Jo.

Or David.

"Get it together, Olive Blackwood," she spat.

Olive wished she could get another take at lunch. But there were no do-overs.

She gave one last exhale and forced herself to get to class. She sailed past Mr. Dodd's "Howdy-you-do, Olive?" and sank into the seat next to Jo. David didn't say anything. He wouldn't even look at her.

When class started, Jo took charge.

"We need to finish our initial plan by Friday. As for filming, we've already agreed on doing interviews, staging a food fight reenactment, and getting footage from our lunch period. Thoughts?"

"My friend's dad was a student here in 1988, and Ms. Cratchett has worked in the lunchroom for over forty years," David said. "They've both agreed to talk with us next week."

"I, um . . . was thinking," Olive mumbled, "we could, um, check the '88 yearbook to see if there was a redheaded student named Fred." She snatched a glance at David. His face appeared unimpressed.

"Nice," Jo said. "Maybe we can get Fred's last name during one of our interviews or from the front office, and then check all the eighties yearbooks for confirmation.

"How about we assign roles? David should conduct the interviews, and I'll direct. Olive, you film."

Olive scowled. In a perfect world, she would've preferred to direct. It was her dream, after all. But the thought of standing up to Jo made it feel like a pile of bricks had collapsed on her chest. Especially with David mad at her. It was easier to keep quiet and go along with Jo's lineup.

"I can tell that you have a suggestion." Jo crossed their arms. "So?"

Olive blushed.

After several slow, uncomfortable seconds, David spoke up.

"How about we take turns? That way we all get to direct, interview, and film."

"Works for me." Jo shrugged. "Olive?"

Olive nodded. She gave David a smile, but it faded when he wouldn't make eye contact.

Jo narrowed their eyes. "What's going on with you two?"

Olive stared at her hands fidgeting in her lap.

"Nothing," David said curtly.

"Oo-kaay." Jo rolled their eyes.

Olive wanted to thank David for suggesting that they all take turns. She wanted to say that she was sorry. But as usual, Olive said nothing.

Chapter Twenty

Worst of All

THE NEXT DAY AT school was just as gut-wrenching.

Olive had gotten a C on her math test. Kayla had kept going on and on about the dreadful Doomsday Dance and valentines invites. In gym, she'd been picked last for basketball. Even though she'd often been open, no one had passed her the ball. Worst of all, David was still ignoring her.

That evening, Jo's father pulled into Olive's driveway. They were going to the Busy Beavers volunteer meeting.

David didn't even acknowledge her as she slid into the back seat. The entire ride, Jo passionately spoke about some lawsuit in Montana.

"There's a group of Gen Z climate activists suing the state for caring more about corporations than their residents. The youngest plaintiff is five years old!"

Olive twisted a lock of hair tight around her finger. As much as she wanted to help save beavers, Olive just didn't want to be there. Not with David mad at her.

"Their testimony talks about how wildfire smoke, heat, and drought have messed up their physical and mental health," Jo continued. "The government should protect their people from climate change!"

Finally, they'd arrived. Jo's dad led them into the Busy Beavers office.

"This place is pretty dingy," Jo huffed.

The dim lighting in the small space highlighted the dark carpet, worn furniture, and yellowed wallpaper. Olive cleaned her glasses on her sweater and slipped them back on. The only semi-interesting thing in the tight space were the few beaver posters on the walls.

Olive hesitated in front of a picture of a large beaver standing on its webbed back feet. The shot zoomed in on its open-mouthed grin. She had an urge to boop its up-close, bulbous nose. That was something Kayla's cat, Twitch, would never let her do.

"That's the infamous Filbert," a deep voiced boomed from behind.

Olive startled and turned to see a slender man with bushy curls and a matching hipster beard.

"That's Oregon Zoo's Stumptown Fil!" David said, bouncing on the balls of his feet. It was the first time today that Olive had heard excitement in his voice. "He's making his prediction next week. I wonder what his forecast will be."

"He's got nothing on Punxsutawney Phil," the slender man said.

"Too bad his track record isn't great," said David. "His first reading was for an early spring, and the zoo had to close early because of snow and ice."

"Even Filbert can't always get it right." The stranger laughed. "I'm Brad Summers, the CEO of Busy Beavers." He shook Mo's hand.

"I'm Mo, and this is my kid, Jo, and their friends, David and Olive."

"Hello!" Jo and David said in unison. Olive gave a slight wave.

"Follow me," Mr. Summers said.

They walked past the empty front desk toward lively chatter down the hall and into a cramped conference room. Barely larger than Olive's bedroom, it smelled like musky vanilla. Frowning, she was reminded of beaver goo. A large wood table sat in the center, taking up most of the space. Jo went straight to the plate of store-bought cookies and grabbed two.

There was hardly anyone there. Olive had pictured a room full of volunteers, talking over one another about the best way to save beavers. Not including the four of them and Mr. Summers, there were only five people, all of them adults. She wasn't sure whether to be disappointed or relieved.

"What brings you guys here?" asked Mr. Summers.

Jo stared at Olive. David looked unsure. Olive's face grew hot.

Unable to speak, Olive focused on her sneakers.

The probability that she'd answer his question out loud? Negative 100 percent. She breathed a sigh of relief when Jo finally jumped in.

"Olive got a video of a neighbor chasing a beaver. And they were waving a frying pan!"

Mr. Summers nodded along. His eyes widened with each new fact.

"Then Olive saw a news report that a beaver was found dead in her neighborhood"—Jo waved their arms—"so we called Oregon Fish and Wildlife to report the chase, but they said it was legal to murder beavers!"

"Wow, that must have been traumatic, Olive," Mr. Summers said, rubbing his beard, "seeing that event."

Olive gave a slight nod.

"I don't know what I would've done in your shoes. That was very brave of you to film it, especially with the neighbor carrying a lethal weapon."

Olive bit her lip.

She slowly locked onto Mr. Summers's kind eyes and warm smile. "Thanks."

Olive swallowed hard. What Jo had said had sparked her interest in helping beavers, but it wasn't why she was here. Then her thoughts landed on Waddle.

"David told us all these cool facts about beavers and . . ." Olive glanced at David, but his attention remained on Mr. Summers. Frowning, she managed to squeak out, "So, I, uh thought I could learn more and, er, put together reels so others can know all the good they do . . . um, so that other beavers don't have to die too."

"That's a wonderful reason," Mr. Summers said. "We're happy to have you here."

Olive couldn't believe how all that had spilled out of her mouth! Her sweaty hands were still shaking. But she'd done it! And he hadn't laughed at her.

"I have an excellent idea." Mr. Summers clapped his hands. "How about the three of you come join us this Saturday? We're holding a rally to bring awareness and support to a petition to ban the hunting and trapping of beavers on Oregon federal land."

"I'm game!" Jo said.

"Me too," David chimed in.

"And, Olive," Mr. Summers said, "I'd love it if you filmed the event. Not only could you use the footage for your reels, but I'd love to post some on our website."

Olive's face lit up, in a good way. "I, uh, yeah . . . I'd like that."

She could finally make a difference. Now if only she could fix things between her and David.

Chapter Twenty-One

A Busy Beaver

DÉJÀ VU WASHED OVER Olive as she slogged through the crowded hall. Feeling queasy, she held her stomach. Someone's backpack whacked her in the shoulder. She was hot and cold and her ears buzzed.

She imagined the scene in her head. An aerial shot where all the other students were blurs pushing past, making Olive appear to be standing still. The only thing faster than the kids in the hall were the thoughts in her head.

I don't wanna go to film I don't wanna face David and Jo I don't know how to make things right. . . .

Olive shook her head, but the thoughts kept coming.

I thought you were cool. It's a harmless nickname. Would you say it to their face . . . ?

Hiking up her heavy backpack, she hurried into class. She tipped her head at Mr. Dodd's greeting, "Happy Friday!" and sank into the seat next to Jo.

"Hey." Olive pushed up her glasses.

"Yo," Jo replied.

Once again, David said nothing.

"Okay, class," Mr. Dodd said. "Every team has received approval for their focus and initial plan. Congratulations! Next week we'll be filming our trailers in the lunchroom. So use this period to figure out your plan of attack."

Excited chatter filled the room. But Olive, Jo, and David remained silent. Jo suspiciously eyed Olive, then David, and Olive again.

Finally, Jo leaned forward and cried, "What's going on with you two?"

Several painful, silent seconds ticked by.

"We're not moving forward as a team until this gets worked out!" Jo grumbled.

"No problem here," David said softly.

Jo pinched the bridge of their nose. "Olive?"

Maybe what's done was done. But Olive didn't want to pretend that everything was okay. She clamped her fists tight in her lap, her nails digging into her palms. Before she could change her mind or even think about what she was doing, Olive squeezed her eyes shut and blurted out, "My best friend and I nicknamed you Mean Vegan Jo!"

Olive heard a gasp and a booming snort-laugh.

She peeked with one eye. David's mouth hung open. Jo doubled over in laughter.

"Honestly?" Jo managed between cackles. "I . . . I kinda like it."

Olive's eyes widened.

"I've definitely been called worse." Jo shrugged.

"Doesn't make it right," said Olive. "I'm sorry."

"Apology accepted." Jo grinned. "We all good?"

Olive nodded.

David smiled. "We're good."

The rest of film class flew by with ease. On Monday, Olive would interview the head of the lunchroom staff, Ms. Cratchett, with David directing. Tuesday, Olive would direct David interviewing his friend's dad who claims to have known redheaded Fred. Unfortunately, Mr. Dodd vetoed their reenactment of a food fight, so Olive had suggested they use online clips instead. And Wednesday, Jo would direct as Olive filmed footage during their lunch period.

While Jo barked about interview questions, Olive snuck out her phone and texted David: I'm sorry. Are we really good?

Her phone buzzed. You're pretty cool, Olive Blackwood.

"Don't forget," Jo's brash voice echoed through the hall, "my dad's picking you up tomorrow. Ten thirty sharp!"

Olive slammed her locker shut. She spun around and gave Jo a thumbs-up.

"Say what?" Kayla's eyebrows shot up.

Kayla nudged again as the two lumbered up the steps onto the school bus. "Thumbs-up for what?"

Olive plopped onto an empty vinyl seat near the

back, setting her heavy backpack on her lap. "Remember that volunteer meeting I went to yesterday? Jo, David, and I are helping at their rally."

"Volunteer meeting? Now a rally?" Kayla shook her head in disbelief. "Aren't you a busy beaver."

Olive chuckled. Now that things were good again with David, she was excited to go. Though she had no intentions of helping with petitions or protests, this was going to be a great opportunity to capture footage about why saving beavers was important.

"Don't be jealous that my social calendar is filling up." Olive giggled.

Full of students and loud chatter, the bus jerked out of the school parking lot.

"Speaking of social calendars"—Kayla playfully shoved Olive's shoulder—"you should ask Bobby to join our group to the V-Day dance."

Olive pressed her lips together. Every time she finally wasn't feeling antsy, Kayla seemed to jab right in a spot that woke up her insecurity. She hadn't even agreed to go with Kayla and her friends. All of whom could dance. Like, ridiculously good.

"Remember, he smiled at you," Kayla pressed on.

Seeing me dance will definitely *turn his smile into laughter.*

"I don't know," Olive mumbled.

"C'mon, what do you got to lose?"

Control. Control. I'm in control.

Avoiding the question, Olive countered with, "Have you asked that eighth grader yet?"

"Sent Jeff the valentine invite today. Oh, I almost forgot," Kayla said. "Can you come over tonight?"

"Say again?" Olive cupped her hand over her ear and leaned in. "You're actually free?"

"Funny. But seriously, I need your help." Kayla nervously ran her hand over her flat-ironed hair. "Remember how I'm leading the dance routine at one of the basketball games?"

Olive nodded.

"We're supposed to use a routine everyone already knows, but now the cocaptains want Abigail and I to add our own signature move at the end.

"I showed a bunch of ideas to Heather and April, but they both seemed underwhelmed. And I'm leading the team in two weeks." Kayla hugged her backpack to her chest. "Two weeks!"

"You mean Jeff's game?" Olive teased in a silly you-like-him voice.

Kayla lightly poked Olive in her side again and again.

Olive moved her torso from side to side, but it was impossible to escape Kayla's attack. "Okay!" she cried. "I'll come over tonight."

With a satisfied smirk, Kayla stopped.

"Because just like beavers, we're partners for life!"

Kayla groaned. "How long do I have to hear about every fact you learn about beavers?"

Olive pretended to pout.

"Kidding." Kayla giggled.

The two intertwined their pinkie fingers, and Kayla said, "Besties for life."

Chapter Twenty-Two

Our Future Depends on It

PANNING HER PHONE OVER the gathering at the Busy Beavers rally, Olive was in her happy place. A space where alarming fears and sweating palms disappeared. She was behind the camera.

After the weak turnout at the volunteer meeting, Olive was shocked over the large crowd. Despite the cold temperatures and light drizzle, there were at least a hundred people at Pioneer Courthouse Square in downtown Portland. And more and more kept stopping by to see what was going on. They were even being visited by local press from KBOO community radio, the *Portland Tribune*, and KATU News!

A local high school marching band played the Oregon State University fight song while their cheer-leading squad rallied the crowd to chant along with revised lyrics:

"Join the fight for
B-E-A-V-E-R-S!
Join!
The!
Fight!
Oregonians, fight, fight, fight!"

Onlookers clapped along with amused grins.

Olive wandered through the crowd, her camera recording, and David by her side. Every so often, they'd stop and David would approach someone for a comment.

"I had no idea beavers were so important to the environment!"

"Climate change is scary. I wanna know how I can help."

"Beavers are so cute!"

Olive bumped David's shoulder and motioned at a lady and her young girl wearing a shirt with the words EARTH DAY IS EVERYDAY across the front.

"May we ask a question on behalf of Busy Beavers?" David waved at Olive's phone.

The mother squeezed her daughter's hand. "If that's okay with you, honey?"

The young girl leaned into her mom and slowly nodded.

"What brings you here today?" David asked.

"We're activists," the girl said softly.

"So are we." David motioned at Olive and himself.

"This one got a bunch of her friends to write letters and draw pictures asking the Oregon Fish and Wildlife to stop allowing the recreational trapping of beavers," the mother said proudly. "She said she did it because beavers can't speak up for themselves."

Olive's brows shot up.

"You did that?" David asked.

"Yup, and we're doing it again." The girl gave a shy smile. "Our future depends on it."

They moved on to interview more attendees when David abruptly stopped. He pulled out his vibrating phone. "Gotta go. Something I promised Mr. Summers I'd help with."

David jogged off before Olive could respond. So she continued filming the scene around her.

There were several tents set up, all with tables manned by a rotation of Busy Beavers employees or volunteers. Some were selling bright red T-shirts, water bottles, and canvas tote bags. They were all decorated with the Busy Beavers logo, a simple outline of the side angle of a beaver with a humped back, large front teeth, and a paddle-shaped tail. They were also selling raffle tickets to win a giant stuffed beaver. The kind usually spotted at impossible-to-win carnival games.

Olive zoomed in on a stack of handouts on one of the tables. Next to pamphlets about Busy Beavers and how to get involved were fliers about the petition going up before the commission in less than two weeks.

OREGON BEAVERS NEED YOUR HELP!
PLEASE CALL OR EMAIL THE OREGON
FISH AND WILDLIFE COMMISSION BEFORE
WEDNESDAY, FEBRUARY 8, AND URGE THEM
TO ACCEPT THE PETITION TO PERMANENTLY
CLOSE BEAVER TRAPPING AND HUNTING ON
THE STATE'S FEDERALLY MANAGED PUBLIC
LANDS AND THE WATERS THAT FLOW
THROUGH THEM.

This petition filed in December by several conservation groups to help save Oregon's official state animal will be voted on during the commission's February 9, 8:00 a.m., meeting. This amendment also helps minimize the impact of climate change, drought, and wildfire.

Beavers are critical to functioning watersheds which benefit hundreds of plants and animals, including threatened and endangered species. Beaver benefits are endless, but most important for all beings is that their way of life mitigates climate change.

Humans made the problem. We need to fix it. One way is to end the cruel practice of beaver hunting and trapping.

For more information about beavers, their positive impact on our planet, or about this petition, please visit the Busy Beavers website.

When Jo had suggested that their documentary team get involved with Busy Beavers, Olive's entire insides had quivered. She'd been too afraid to say that she didn't want to go. It was the one time her dizzying fear had worked in her favor!

Though it didn't change the fact that she hadn't spoken up sooner about the beaver chase, and she knew it wouldn't bring Waddle back, Olive was proud of herself for doing something now.

During the last hour of the rally, Jo sat at one of the tables handing out pamphlets and fliers. Olive lingered behind them, reviewing her footage from the day.

"Hey, I'm Vicky Goldmann. Is David Moore around?"

Olive looked up from her screen.

A short, pretty blond, surrounded by a group of kids, stood in front of Jo. She smiled big, showing off her metal braces. "We're all in environmental club together."

"He's doing what he does best." Jo pointed to the center of the public square.

Olive gasped.

The band was playing some kid's song about counting and beavers as a human-sized brown beaver pranced around to the beat. It was their middle school mascot, Leevitt the Beaver—aka David! Olive quickly started filming. She moved closer for a better shot.

Instead of being covered in rich, dense fur, the costume appeared velvety soft. His cartoonish face had large brown eyes, a wide black nose with whiskers hanging downward, and a bucktoothed grin. He turned around and wiggled his broad, flattened tail. The crowd roared with excitement. Kids pointed and giggled. Olive's eyes widened.

She couldn't believe that the usually quiet, unmemorable David Moore was dazzling everyone with his smooth dance moves. There was a whole extraordinary, in-your-face side to David that she'd known nothing about!

As the crowd sang, "Stop! It's Beaver Time," David moonwalked across the brick concrete. He continued dancing while the crowd shouted, "Go, beaver! Go, beaver!"

The mother and daughter they'd interviewed earlier caught Olive's attention. The two were dancing and laughing and having fun. Olive couldn't stop wondering how someone so young and so shy could be so brave.

Once the performance ended, Olive noticed the Busy Beavers CEO up ahead.

"Mr. Summers!" she called.

He turned, staring into the crowd with a confused look.

Olive's breath quickened.

What am I doing?

He smiled once he saw Olive waving.

Her heartbeat raced.

What was I thinking?

"So glad you could make it!" He pointed at Olive's phone. "Get some good footage?"

Olive nodded.

Control. You can do this, Olive Blackwood. Control.

"Could I . . . uh." Olive's shaky voice squeaked. "Ask a question or two?"

"Of course!"

Olive slowly raised her phone and hit record.

You got this, Olive Blackwood.

"Can you, um, talk about why, uh, beavers are so important?"

"I'd love to," Mr. Summers said, rubbing his beard. "They're excellent hydro engineers, and they'll figure out ways around just about everything! Water doesn't always go where we want it to, but beavers have a way of getting water to work for them. . . ."

Olive beamed as he continued talking about the keystone species and their amazing benefits.

I'm doing it! I'm taking action for Waddle! Because beavers can't speak up for themselves.

Chapter Twenty-Three

The Cursor Is Mightier than the Frying Pan

OLIVE SAT TALL IN her director's chair. Finally, she was in control.

She'd spent over an hour putting together her first KidVid reel. It wasn't her best work, but there wasn't much time. The Oregon Fish and Wildlife Commission was voting in ten days.

The faster she got the word out, the quicker people could take action.

Hopefully, her post would convince others to contact

the commission before their decision. Beavers' lives were literally at stake, and for once, she wasn't afraid to do something about it. At least in her own way.

Using the video-editing app, Quick Clip, Olive had cut and joined together footage from the Lone Fir Cemetery, the neighborhood beaver chase, and the Busy Beavers rally videos. She watched it one last time before posting.

The reel started with a clip of the old lady chasing Waddle, her face hidden behind the wicked-witch sticker. An animated version of Olive dropped into the scene. She swung a yellow-bladed lightsaber, blocking the old lady's path.

Suddenly, a murder of cawing crows flew across the screen, then faded to black. Adventure orchestral music blared as the title THE CURSOR IS MIGHTIER THAN THE FRYING PAN scrolled backward in a star-filled sky. Just like the *Star Wars* opening crawl effect, followed by:

OREGON BEAVERS NEED YOUR HELP! EVEN THOUGH THEY'RE THE STATE ANIMAL, IT'S LEGAL TO "TAKE"—AKA KILL—BEAVERS IN

OREGON. WE MAY BE TOO YOUNG TO VOTE,
BUT WE CAN STILL MAKE A DIFFERENCE!

CONTACT THE COMMISSION BEFORE
FEBRUARY 9, AND TELL THEM TO ACCEPT
THE PETITION TO CLOSE BEAVER TRAPPING
AND HUNTING ON OREGON FEDERAL LAND
FOREVER!

NO MORE EXTERMINATING BEAVERS!

SHARE WITH FRIENDS, PARENTS,
TEACHERS, AND NEIGHBORS. TOGETHER WE
CAN SAVE THE BEAVERS AND THE PLANET!

A cartoon beaver waddled across the screen transitioning into clips from the rally. Using snippets from her interview, a voice-over from Mr. Summers explained why passing this petition not only benefited beavers, but all nature, including humans.

The video switched back to the old lady chasing Waddle, when—*poof!*—a cloud of smoke filled the screen. When it disappeared, the animated image of Olive dressed in a magician's robe stood in its place. She pushed up her red glasses and pointed her wand possessed with a manticore's claws. Saying the magic word, *Control*, a protection bubble surrounded the beaver.

The final image was a close-up of Waddle and the text SAVE THE BEAVERS, SAVE THE PLANET, along with a link to send the commission an email.

Seconds after posting, Olive's tablet pinged again and again!

There was a long way to go before matching the reaction to the beaver-chase video—now at over eight thousand likes! But the ninety-second reel was doing exactly what she'd hoped.

Olive read some of the comments:

Why would anyone wanna kill
beavers?!
Message to the commission sent.
Reducing wildfires and drought?
Beavers are magicians!

They're the cutest engineers I've ever
seen.
I give a dam about beavers!
Sounds like they're the key to saving
humanity.

Kids, like herself before Waddle, hadn't known about all the good beavers did for the environment. And now that they did, together they could make a difference.

Olive replied to her post: *Our voice matters. Our future, our planet, depends on it.*

Cut!

LIFE WAS PRETTY GOOD for a Monday.

Kayla hadn't mentioned the Doomsday Dance or Bobby. Not one teacher had called on her. There had been no pop quizzes. And not once had she felt nauseous. She'd even been picked first for dodgeball in gym! Even if it was by David.

Jo, David, and Olive strolled toward film class.

"Love your latest KidVid post," David said.

"Your reels are pretty dope," Jo agreed.

Olive beamed. Her first reel encouraging users to contact the commission had reached almost two thousand likes! She'd posted another one last night to keep the momentum going. Her goal was to post one every single night until the day of the vote.

"I have an idea for more footage," David said. "Catching them in their natural environment!"

Olive frowned in confusion.

"Beaver watching! I've done it lots of times with my parents to help with beaver surveys to monitor dams and other activity."

"Cool," Olive said.

"I'm in!" said Jo.

"And if you want"—David began to strut—"come see me do my mascot thing at the basketball game Wednesday?"

Jo snort-laughed and turned to Olive. "Sounds like you'll be getting all kinds of film. You in?"

Olive hiked up her backpack. She knew nothing and wanted to know nothing about sports. The potential to do something embarrassing in front of who knew how many students was exponential.

What if I call out the wrong thing?

What if I cheer when everyone else is silent?

What if I slip and fall on the slick gymnasium floor?

But then Olive considered that she could get more great footage of David wowing the crowd. Plus, Jo hadn't been *that* intense lately. The two were sorta-kinda becoming friends.

Olive finally grinned. "Count me in!"

"What's up, Doc!?" Mr. Dodd said in a bad Bugs Bunny impersonation as the trio walked into the lunchroom.

"Hey, Mr. Dodd," they sang, and joined the other classmates huddled near the door.

The place felt huge without the usual chaos of students and echoing chatter. The stench of bleach masked their three-bean chili lunch. The empty tables and linoleum floors gleamed. Cubicle walls had been set up, dividing the space into six areas.

After the bell rang, Mr. Dodd clapped his hands for attention.

"What did the janitor say when he jumped out of the closet?" He paused, smiling. "Supplies!"

Groans rumbled. Jo chuckled.

"All right," Mr. Dodd said. "Today we start filming!"

Hoots and hollers bounced off the walls.

"This will show you where your team's been assigned." Mr. Dodd waved a piece of paper and posted it onto the wall. Students rushed forward. Olive lingered behind the mob. "To accommodate different areas of access, make sure to check this every day at the start of class.

"Feel free to ask questions at any time. But most important, have fun!"

Olive followed David and Jo to the partitioned area near the register. Ms. Cratchett was already waiting for them.

The lunchroom supervisor wore her usual pressed uniform top and loose khaki pants, but the apron was gone. She looked different with her auburn curly bob not hidden under a hairnet.

"Hi, Ms. Cratchett," David said. "Like we already discussed, Olive will do the interview, I'll direct, and Jo will film."

Ms. Cratchett smirked. "Jo and I know one another very well."

"Hey, Miss C." Jo lifted their chin.

Olive took out her notebook and searched for their questions. Her hands wouldn't stop shaking. Muscles tense, she rubbed the back of her neck. She was starting to wish that they'd stuck with Jo's original lineup. Filming she was great at. Speaking, not so much.

David dragged a chair away from a table and placed it in front of the wall.

"Ms. Cratchett"—David waved at the seat—"why don't you sit here?"

He placed another chair facing the first. "Jo, this spot is for you to get a head-on shot."

Jo gave a thumbs-up.

"And, Olive, you'll stand behind Jo."

Whew, she wouldn't be on camera. Unfortunately, her stomach still fluttered.

Ms. Cratchett fluffed her curls, then rested her hands in her lap.

"Action!" David said.

"Um," Olive squeaked, "please, uh, tell us—"

"Cut!" David turned to Olive. "Try projecting your voice with credibility and confidence. You know, like a news reporter."

Olive nodded, her face growing hot.

David leaned into her and whispered, "Do you need a minute?"

She swallowed hard. She considered fleeing to the bathroom. Or just leaving school all together.

Why can't I do this? It's only David and Jo and Ms. Cratchett. Control, control, control.

The flutter in her belly thudded harder. Taking a deep breath, she thought about the rally. The shy girl activist, David dancing as Leevitt the Beaver, and her interview with Mr. Summers.

Control, Olive Blackwood. You can do this.

"No," she said forcefully.

David smiled. "Action!"

Olive stood tall. "Please tell us your name and occupation."

I did it, I did it, I did it!

She shook her shoulders with excitement while Ms. Cratchett answered, then followed up with the next question. "Are you familiar with the Food Fight of 1988?"

"I'm not only familiar, but I was here when it

happened," she said. "Most people are surprised to learn that Fred is real.

"Real sweet kid. Shy but sweet."

I got this, I got this, I got this!

The next day was Olive's turn to direct.

Her butterflies were back, but after two successful interviews in a row, she was sure she could handle directing a quick conversation with a parent. Olive was 40, 50 percent confident.

Mr. Dodd set their team in a back corner with access to a school laptop.

"Since David will be interviewing his friend's dad virtually, we'll just use the screen recorder," said Olive. "That way there won't be any glare issues or the phone's reflection on the screen."

"What am I supposed to do?" Jo pursed their lips.

Olive shrugged.

David smiled big. "Be your most awesome, supportive self?"

"You got it." Jo smirked.

David sat in front of the computer and pulled up the

video conference. An old guy dressed in a business suit was already waiting.

"Hi, Mr. Miller!" David waved. "These are my teammates, Olive and Jo."

They crowded around David until their faces appeared on the screen.

"Hey, guys. Happy to be helping out."

"David will ask some questions, you'll answer, and that's it," Jo said. "Easy peasy!"

Olive exhaled loudly.

"And Olive here will be directing," Jo quickly added and stepped aside.

Olive waved. "Can you, uh, move over a bit, Mr. Miller? Position yourself so you're dead center."

Mr. Miller scooted over. "This good?"

"Perfect," Olive's voice squeaked. "Everyone ready?"

Mr. Miller and David nodded.

"To do nothing," Jo mumbled.

Olive rolled her eyes. "Action."

"Please tell us your name and how you're connected to Cascadia Middle School," David said.

"My name's Robert Miller, and I was a student at

Cascadia in the eighties. From 1987 to '91."

"Have you heard of the Food Fight—"

"Cut!" Jo cried.

Olive stomped her foot. "Jo!"

"You never started recording," Jo said.

"Oh." Olive's cheeks blazed. She pulled up the software, then hesitated. Her stomach churned. "Uh, I'll be right back."

With Mr. Dodd's permission, Olive raced to the bathroom. Two eighth graders stood in front of the mirrors, touching up their makeup. Glaring, they stopped talking. Olive's teeth began to chatter. She locked herself in a stall.

Their conversation resumed. But Olive's thoughts drowned them out.

Please don't get sick. Not here. Not now. Control, control, control.

Time dragged on. With each passing minute, Olive's heartbeat pounded harder and faster.

Ugh, what am I doing? I need to get back to class.

What kind of director hides in a bathroom stall? I'm such a loser.

Finally, the two girls left. Thankfully, Olive hadn't been hit with a sneaky poop attack.

She checked her phone and gasped. She'd be gone for over ten minutes!

She quickly washed her face and rushed back to class. The computer screen was black.

"Where's Mr. Miller?" Olive asked.

"He had a work meeting," said David. "So we did the interview while you were gone."

"Oh."

"No biggie," Jo said. "There wasn't any acting, so directing wasn't really necessary."

Though relieved, Olive's cheeks still stung.

"Everything okay?" David asked.

Olive nodded. But her cramps still lingered.

They played the interview for Olive. Mr. Miller's description of the food fight matched Ms. Cratchett's story. He'd also shared that Fred was no redhead. Instead, he'd sported a fly high-top fade with a flattop standing at almost eight inches tall!

Fred had recently transferred and had been picked on by some eighth graders. Fed up, Fred had torpedoed his creamed corn at them. He'd hit some girl named Libby—*not* Lizzy—instead. The bullies had launched a counterattack with mashed potatoes and peas. After being dragged to the principal's office, no one ever saw Fred at school again.

"Nice," Olive said flatly.

She wanted to be excited. Their project was going great. But once again, the negative chatter returned. *This is a nightmare. I can't direct. Maybe this dream was never meant for me.*

Chapter Twenty-Five

Good Things Come in Pink Boxes

KAYLA LINKED HER ARM with Olive's and dragged her toward the hot pink building. "If Voodoo Doughnut doesn't make you feel better, I don't know what will."

A beat-up coin-operated kiddie ride sat by the entrance. The stained-glass windows surrounding the front door flaunted colorful signature doughnuts, including the iconic voodoo doll stabbed with a pretzel stake. So far, Olive wasn't feeling better.

Inside, a group of teens huddled around a pinball

machine. Insistent dings pierced Olive's ears as the score kept rising. Funky junk from a carousel horse to a velvet painting of some country singer took up space.

Olive sighed. As usual, the line was long, mainly with annoying tourists.

Pink box in hand, Kayla snagged an open bench shaped like a coffin. Olive slumped down across from her.

Kayla opened the box and took out her favorite, the Memphis Mafia.

She waved a plastic knife. "Split it?"

Olive eyed the treat covered in chocolate chips, peanuts, and chocolate and peanut butter drizzle. She shrugged.

"All right, sourpuss," Kayla said, carefully cutting the fried dough stuffed with banana chunks. "So the interview didn't go well. You'll do—"

"The interview went fine"—Olive hung her head in her hands—"after I left."

"Like I was saying, you'll do better next time." She slid half of the doughnut toward Olive.

"I suck at directing!" Olive wailed.

"Pssh!" Kayla argued. "You've directed my brothers and me hundreds of times. You're great!"

"That's just it," Olive said. "I've *only* directed you guys. I'm too freaked out to direct anyone else." Her body shook. But she still kept going. "It's why I didn't want to direct your dance team friends. It's just, I guess . . . directing's not my dream anymore." Olive's eyes began to water.

"Yes, you're shy," Kayla said softly. "But you're also awesome. Look at everything you've done recently. You interviewed that CEO at the rally, and your KidVid reels have been blowing up! You're an influencer now!"

Olive gave a sad smile.

"Seriously," Kayla said, holding Olive's gaze. "I'm super proud of you. I'm sure Waddle is too. So what if directing isn't your dream career anymore? Maybe you'll write scripts or produce or something else. The possibilities are endless."

Slowly, Olive's stomach pains and chills began to fade. She stared at the shop's famous saying printed on the doughnut box. *Good Things Come in Pink Boxes.*

Kayla broke off a chunk of her doughnut half and

held it up. "Do you think Jo believes that Voodoo has decent vegan options?" She popped the piece in her mouth.

Olive giggled.

Good things do *come in neon shirts with loud opinions and beaver-mascot costumes.*

"Just so you know"—Kayla twirled the end of one of her side pigtails tight around her finger—"we all have bad days."

Olive frowned as Kayla's shining eyes grew dark.

"I really have doubts about making cocaptain." Kayla's voice was low and shaky. "I kind of want to give up and let Abigail have it."

"What? No!" Olive slapped her palms on the tabletop. "You're super talented and deserve to be cocaptain. Don't give the spot away. Make her work for it!"

Kayla nodded. But the light in her eyes was still missing.

"Maybe we could do our Make It Come True spell?" Olive suggested.

Kayla shook her head. "That feels like making someone's decision for them.

"But you're right."

"I am?" Olive pushed up her glasses.

"I *am* a good dancer." Kayla's sparkle was back. "And I'm *not* giving away my chance at cocaptain." She held out her pinkie.

And great things happen with magical best friends.

The two intertwined their pinkies and said, "Besties for life."

Leevitt the Beaver

OLIVE WAS DOING THE unthinkable.

Instead of sitting at home alone watching a fantasy film, she sat in the bleachers at the school gym. Surrounded by fans wearing the school colors, brown and orange, excited chatter echoed off the walls. She was squished between Jo and some kid who definitely *wasn't* familiar with deodorant.

The most unbelievable part? Olive was enjoying herself.

The Cascadia school band began blasting a familiar pop tune. Olive bounced her head along. Kids still trickled into the gym before game time. Olive caught sight of Bobby Filmore.

And he was heading in her direction!

She squeezed her sweaty palms together, wishing that Kayla was by her side.

Bobby climbed up the steps with this other kid Olive recognized from science class. Her heartbeat sped up. As they walked past, Bobby said, "Sup."

Olive inhaled deep . . . and smiled! At least she thought she had and hadn't only wished it to happen. She whipped out her phone and immediately texted Kayla: Bobby said SUP to me!!!

But then her nerves started creeping in.

Ugh, why did I text Kayla? Now she'll never let up on sending him a valentine! Control, Olive Blackwood. Must learn—

A trumpet blasted, disturbing Olive's spiraling thoughts.

The cheerleading squad strutted out onto the court. Leevitt the Beaver waddled out behind them. Olive immediately hit record and zeroed in on David. He kicked out his webbed feet. One at a time, over and over, going faster and faster with the band's beat.

Even after his performance at the rally last weekend, Olive was still blown away at this side of David. He turned and wiggled his beaver tail. The crowd cheered.

Once the band finished, the cheerleaders led everyone in a chant:

"WE ARE THE BEAVERS
AND WE CAN'T BE BEAT.
WE GOT THE POWER
TO KNOCK YA OFF YOUR FEET!"

David bounced around, shaking his hips. He gave high fives to fans in the stands.

Jo leaned into Olive. "Look at him go!"

"He's pretty cool." Olive grinned.

Five of the Beavers' players gathered in the center of the court along with five from the other team. A shrill whistle sounded and the referee tossed the ball into the air. Jeff, the eighth grader Kayla had sent the valentine invite to, leaped up and easily tapped it toward his teammates.

Jeff made the first shot. Everyone—including Olive—jumped to their feet, shouting, "Go, Beavers, go!"

Sneakers squeaked back and forth across the court. Cheers followed whenever they sunk the shot, or groans whenever they missed. The referee blew his whistle and held out both arms straight in front of him, palms facing outward. Not sure what was going on, Olive's eyebrows scrunched together.

"Jeff made a personal foul when he bumped into the other team's player," Jo explained. "Now they get two free throws."

Still confused, Olive just nodded.

Bouncing the ball, the opponent's petite player stared at the basket with a determined glare. Everyone stomped their feet. The bleachers shook. He missed his shot! The gym filled with thunderous applause, and again when he missed the second.

By the end of the second quarter, Beavers were ahead 18–9.

Despite not understanding the game and the sore backside from the metal benches, Olive wondered why she'd never come to games before. It was so much fun!

The Cascadia dance team jogged out onto the court. They wore matching black leggings and bright orange sparkling tops. Abigail stood center in the front line with six girls. Olive spotted Kayla in the back.

Just like all the other times her best friend had performed for recitals and competitions, Kayla looked dope. She wore deep purple lipstick and shimmering eyeshadow. Her hair was parted down the middle with six tight braids close to her scalp, every other cornrow dyed orange.

Thumping bass began to play so loud, Olive could feel it in her chest. All twelve girls broke into a synchronized routine to the mash-up of funky pop songs. Whistles and whoops filled the air.

That's when it hit Olive.

Of course, she'd never been to a game before. With Kayla always performing, she'd never had anyone to go with. The idea of sitting here alone with all eyes on her, the lonely dork clapping offbeat, made her teeth clench.

Must learn control.

That's not me anymore. I'm not here alone. And I'm cheering on TWO friends.

I'm in control.

Leevitt sprang back onto the court. Olive shoved aside her thoughts and swiped her phone from her lap. She began recording again.

The dancers stood around Leevitt in a semicircle, clapping as he broke into a solo routine. He cycled through several old-school hip-hop moves. Ending with a nod to break dance, he spun on his back. Cheers flooded the gym.

The squad resumed their coordinated dance, their final move, a pop-and-lock routine.

Olive pointed at Kayla. "That's my best friend, Kayla."

"Go, Kayla!" Jo hollered.

Feeling brave next to Jo, Olive joined in.

"Go, Kayla!" Olive shrieked.

Kayla flashed a bright smile.

Abigail made a face as if she'd smelled something rotten and stumbled off beat. She quickly recovered with a toothy grin.

Halftime ended with the cheerleaders tossing out school mascot shirts to the crowd and Jo snagging one. The game ended with Jeff making the last shot right as the buzzer went off and then chest-bumped with David! Beavers slayed 32–18!

A dozen kids rushed down the bleachers to join the team, the cheerleaders, the dance squad, and of course, Leevitt the Beaver. They all jumped up and down, yelling, "Beavers can't be beat!" The band played "We Are the Champions" as the rest of the crowd spilled onto the court.

As the excitement began to wind down and the crowd strolled out of the gym, Olive and Jo joined Kayla and Abigail.

"Sup." Kayla gave Olive a wink.

Olive cringed.

"Y'all the cheerleaders?" Jo asked.

Abigail made a sour face. "We're on the dance team. The cheerleaders are more preppy meets peppy, while we have more attitude and sass."

Jo cocked an eyebrow. "Oo-kaay."

"We both bring spirit to games"—Kayla made jazz hands—"but we don't chant. We dance."

"Speaking of spirit"—Abigail tossed her hair like she was filming an influencer video—"what was that screeching during our routine, Olive? Thought you were dying or something."

Olive's cheeks burned.

"Aaabii," Kayla said in that take-it-down-a-notch tone. "My girl's just got my back is all."

"We were cheering for Kayla"—Jo smirked—"since she had the best attitude and sass."

Olive and Kayla exchanged surprised looks.

"Anyways." Abigail released a bored sigh. "Later, Kayla."

Kayla hugged Olive and squealed. "I'm so glad you came!"

"You smashed it!" Olive said. "Cocaptain is yours."

"I hope so." Kayla rubbed her neck. "Hearing your voice really got me out of my head and back into the routine."

"I can't take all the credit." Olive shrugged. "Jo started it."

"Thanks, Jo," Kayla said.

"Yeah, thanks, Jo." Olive beamed.

This whole time, Olive had thought that David was this unmemorable kid. But between all his beaver knowledge and smooth mascot moves, she'd been wrong. She'd also thought that Jo was scary. Sure, Jo was bold, loud, and often in your face. But they'd just stood up to Abigail for her and Kayla. And they weren't afraid to step in and speak up when Olive or David couldn't.

Worst of all, Olive hadn't believed in herself.

Over the past week, however, Olive had pushed past her comfort zone again and again.

She puffed out her chest. *You did it, Olive Blackwood. You took action.*

Not only had she spoken up for beavers, but she'd also gone to her first basketball game!

But most of all, Olive was proud of being friends with Kayla, David, and Jo.

Chapter Twenty-Seven

"May Me Beefur"

"IT'S THE BEST DAY ever!" David sang like SpongeBob. "Beaver watching, beaver watching, beaver watching, beaver watching!"

Olive caught an amused grin flare across Jo's face.

They stood outside at the pickup area in front of the school parking lot. David and Jo had come fully prepared for tonight's beaver watching—filled water bottle, binoculars, and a headlamp. Olive, on the other hand, was obviously a novice to wandering around in nature in the dark.

Olive stared at Jo's not-typical-for-school tools. She wished she was a fan of horror movies so she'd have been better equipped.

"My parents and I sometimes go camping. Not at all my thing, but . . ." Jo shrugged.

"Sorry I forgot to tell you about the necessary gear." David grimaced. "But don't worry. My parents always have extra stuff in the trunk. Except don't count on any binoculars. My dad would never leave his six-hundred-dollar pair in the car."

Olive's brows shot up. Six hundred dollars? They must be super-long-distance and see-through-brick-walls type of binoculars!

Hit with a gust of wind, Olive pulled up her hood and cinched it tight. The only thing she'd gotten right was bundling up. Though it was above freezing, once the sun went down, it was sure to fall into the high thirties.

David's parents pulled up in a small SUV. They all piled into the back seat with David in the middle. Thankfully, David was right, and there was an extra headlamp and water bottle in the trunk. After scarfing down a quick meal and filling up the empty bottle for

Olive at Burgerville, they took off for Tideman Johnson City Park.

Fifteen minutes later, they pulled near the park's entrance with the engine still running. David's dad turned around to face all three in the back seat.

"Okay, kids," Mr. Moore said, "have fun and stick together. David has done this a hundred times before, so just follow his lead."

David's cheeks reddened, but he raised his chin.

Mrs. Moore glanced at the digital clock on the dashboard. "It's almost four forty-five, so you have about a half hour until sunset. Then an hour until sundown. We'll be back to pick you up at eight thirty, but text if you're ready earlier or need anything. Okay?"

"Yes, Mrs. Moore," Olive and Jo said in unison at the same time David said, "Yes, Mom."

They all jumped out of the van, put on their backpacks, and secured their headlamps around their heads. They exited the parking lot and onto the paved trail. Olive took out her phone and hit the record button. There would be lots of editing ahead, but she didn't want to miss anything! Before long, Olive heard rushing water, and soon they intersected with Johnson Creek.

David stepped off the trail onto an unpaved path. "Don't be disappointed if we don't see any beavers."

Olive frowned. Of course, she'd be upset. The whole point of this adventure was to get them on film and share it with the KidVid community!

More than ever, she wanted to spread the word about how awesome beavers were for the environment. And that they too deserved a place to live with their family. A safe place where they didn't have to worry about humans. Especially those with frying pans.

"Sometimes it takes a while for the animals to get used to your presence," David continued, "before they let themselves be seen."

With David in front, the three crept alongside the water in a single file line. Olive faced the camera to capture the meandering creek. Her free fingers went up to her forehead and grazed the smooth strap. Tapping the plastic light, she felt ridiculous with this headlamp on.

The trees and brush grew thicker around them as they kept hiking. Rocks crunched underneath their heavy steps. A slow, sweet trill whistled above. Olive held her camera up overhead but didn't catch sight of the bird.

Olive thought it strange that David's head hung low rather than facing forward. But Olive trusted in what Mr. Moore had said, that David knew what he was doing. Nocturnal mammals, beavers go out at sundown and return home at dawn, so finding a spot near a beaver's lodge by sunset was their goal.

David paused and waved at the tree stump to his right. "This is beaver chew! You can tell by the—"

"Wait!" Olive swung her phone to capture both David and the stump in her shot. "Now start over."

David let out an exhale and began again.

"This is beaver chew—"

"No, no," Olive said. "With the same excitement as before!"

"Hurry up," Jo huffed. "It's almost sunset!"

"This is beaver chew!" David smiled too big, but Olive let him finish. "Beaver-chewed bark has distinct grooves from their teeth and come out to a sharp point, while branches cut by humans are usually flat. You can tell the difference by running your fingers against the cuts."

Olive zoomed in as David demonstrated and pointed out the teeth marks. He continued walking alongside the creek until he spotted something in the water. "Look!"

Olive followed his gaze to the long line of piled rocks and thin branches balancing on top.

"Beavers often use rocks as a base for their dams. This is either the remains of an old one or a new one under construction. We're not far now!" He hustled on.

As her breath quickened, Olive tried her best to steady her camera.

"There's the beaver den," David whispered with excitement.

Olive zeroed in on the large pile of sticks covered with lots of green shrubs on the creek's bank, just above calm waters.

"And now," David said, taking out a paper bag from his backpack, "an offering for the beavers."

He pulled out a halved apple and tossed it into the water. He handed both Olive and Jo each an apple half. They threw their halves into the creek. David pushed on, veering away from the water, with Olive and Jo in tow.

He came to an abrupt stop. "This is it. The place where we wait."

"Can't we get closer to the water?" Olive squinted toward the den's opening, trying to make out a shadow that had moved in the distance. She didn't want to miss her chance to capture a beaver on film. Though they weren't that far away, Olive worried about being able to see anything, even with their headlamps on.

David shook his head. "We should stay at least fifteen feet away."

"How about we hide out here?" Jo waved behind a cluster of tall trees.

"No point," David said. "Beavers may have poor eyesight, but they have excellent hearing and sense of smell."

David settled onto the ground and said, "The most important thing is to sit still and keep quiet. That way the animals will ignore us. Remember, no flash and no light when taking pictures or filming." David stared at Olive.

Jo sat cross-legged next to David. Olive slipped off her backpack and plopped down next to Jo. Thankfully, Olive had remembered to charge her phone. They had almost three hours before David's parents were picking them up. She pulled out her tripod and set up her phone in front of her.

Almost an hour had passed as the three sat in silence. The sun had fully disappeared. With no city lights it was pitch dark and creepily still. To be less distracting to wildlife, all three switched on the red-light option on their headlamps. Using night vision mode, Olive continued to film.

Her backside started to fall asleep. Olive rocked back and forth, trying to get rid of the tingling numbness.

Slowly, the park was waking up. Frogs croaked. Something scurried nearby. With every rustle, chirp, and squeak, Jo jumped.

Suddenly, a siren blared, and a coyote howled in the distance. Jo grabbed Olive's hand. Several other coyotes joined in. Jo nervously switched on their cell phone light *and* a flashlight that Olive hadn't realized they'd had.

"Turn those off," David said in a forceful whisper.

Olive squeezed Jo's hand. They squeezed back and turned off both lights.

Olive couldn't believe that the very tough, very loud,

and very confident Jo was afraid of the dark! Even Olive was used to hearing coyotes when her and Kayla had visited Aunt T in the suburbs.

Just like Kayla's nerves with trying out for cocaptain, Olive realized that *everyone*—even those who were bold—was afraid of something.

The next time Jo grabbed her hand, they were signaling to Olive about a possible sighting. That's when Olive heard some loud tail slaps.

Olive slowly scanned the creek from left to right and back again. She gasped. There were ripples on the surface. She zoomed in with her camera. But couldn't make out anything.

Jo handed her their binoculars. Olive saw nothing and offered them back. But Jo waved it away. Olive gave a sheepish grin and resumed her watch.

After several breath-holding moments, Jo poked Olive and then pointed to David.

David mouthed something.

What? Olive mouthed back.

He mouthed again, but she still had no clue what David was trying to say. It looked sort of like *May Me*

Beefur. Eee. Olive doubted that that was what he was saying.

Unfortunately, Olive had never been great at lip-reading. The first time Kayla had tried to tell her something from across the classroom in second grade, Olive had shouted, "What?!" The two had gotten into trouble for talking in class.

David slowly, one more time, mouthed the words, and it finally clicked. *Baby beavers! Kits!*

Using the binoculars, Olive scanned the water again. She noticed what looked like a drifting log or . . . Olive released a soft, happy "Eek." It was a beaver! Wait, no, it was *two* beavers.

Two kits were playing in the creek!

Olive quickly made sure her camera was capturing this amazing moment. They appeared to be doing some kind of weird wrestle dance in dark sludge, two pairs of glowing eyes bobbing along. They paused their tussle. Their front paws intertwined, they floated leisurely in the calm water.

Olive's lips parted. Even if she had words, nothing could be said to capture the intensity of the scene before her. She had a strong urge to move closer, but she didn't want to disturb their play.

The kits' sparring dance resumed. More wiggling and twirling and bopping up and down until one was backed into a corner. Eventually they dove underwater and were gone.

Olive, David, and Jo remained frozen in awe, lingering in this magical moment.

Chapter Twenty-Eight

Guaranteed Impending Doom

KAYLA PLOPPED ONTO OLIVE'S bed with a dramatic sigh.

"I can't believe my mom scheduled a doctor's appointment next week. On the *exact* day that I lead the dance team! And it's in Salem!" Kayla fell back with a grunt. "SALEM! What if we don't make it back in time?"

"It's not that far away," Olive said.

"That's what she said, but you know how ugly traffic can get."

Kayla covered her head with a pillow and groaned loudly.

"It's gonna be okay." Olive tugged on Kayla's sock-covered foot hanging off the bed. She waited for a response but the only sound in the room was Jonáe's song playing in the background. This one about female frenemies. When the song ended, Olive tried again.

"Seriously. You'll get back in time for the game, and you'll rock the routine. There'll be a standing ovation, and everything will be fine. Remember, the Sacred Skittles said so!"

Kayla slid off the bed and picked up their Book of Enchantment from the dresser. She laid it on the floor next to Olive, opened to the page titled "The Future Is as Sweet as Candy," and sat facing Olive.

Without a word, Olive scrambled to her dresser. She dug through the top drawer until she found a fun-sized bag of M&M's and one for Skittles. She grabbed two plates and a candle, switched off the music, and settled back onto the floor.

Kayla shook the Skittles bag over her plate. "Will I be the new dance team cocaptain?"

Olive had hoped that her reassuring words had reached Kayla. And that she would've asked about something else instead. Why mess with a "destined to win" answer? Especially since Kayla was practicing nonstop and had chosen—and perfected—her signature move.

Of course, one truth about reading futures was that nothing was set in stone. Aunt T had taught them that predictions were all based on where everything stood in the moment the question was asked. The future could always change. Because everyone has free will. The freedom to change their feelings, perspective, and actions, affecting everything around them.

Aunt T had also said, however, to not keep asking the same question over and over. At some point, you had to trust the guidance given and then follow your gut. As simple as magic could be, it was also confusing.

Kayla tore open the bag and a shower of Skittles clanked onto the dish. Studying the candies, Kayla gasped. There wasn't one strawberry-flavored Skittle.

"Outlook hazy," Kayla whispered.

"That's not so bad," Olive said.

Kayla gave her a look.

"I mean, it's not impending doom so, there's still a chance to make cocaptain."

"It's your go," Kayla said.

Olive wished there were something she could say to make Kayla feel better. Like that Kayla was ten times better at dance than Abigail and ten million times nicer. But she knew that Kayla didn't want to hear it from her. She wanted the Sacred Skittles to confirm what it had already predicted.

Olive also understood how it felt to not get the answer you were hoping for. They had documented their results every time they'd read their futures over the years. There were only two times when the candies had been wrong.

The first was in the fourth grade when Kayla had asked if Ken really liked her. The Skittles had predicted "destined to win." But a week later during recess, Ken had screamed, "You stink!" and shoved her to the ground.

The second time happened last school year. Olive had asked if Bobby would ask her to dance. The Magic M&M's had lied with its "destined to win" response.

Olive shook her fun-sized M&M's bag and decided to follow Kayla's lead.

"Will I get Mr. Dodd's personal recommendation for Rose City?"

Olive stared intently as the M&M's rolled around on her plate. Everything was going so great with her team project that she had to know if there'd been any progress in changing her "hazy outlook."

Unable to look away, Olive felt nauseous.

Not only were there more yellow candies than any other color—her least favorite color—but almost all the pieces were turned so that the *m* wasn't showing.

Kayla sucked in her breath.

Olive couldn't believe it. Guaranteed impending doom.

Without a word, Olive closed the book of spells and set it back on the dresser. She dumped her M&M's in the trash.

"Movie?" she said flatly.

Kayla nodded.

They spent the rest of the evening watching *Enchanted* for the umpteenth time. It was the one movie that they had both loved since they were little. It had romance for Kayla. Fantasy for Olive. And, of course, they were both giddy over anything with magic. Now that they were older, it was obviously cheesy but still just as comforting. Even when the princess-to-be was sent away from animated magical land to our world—the place "where there were no happily-ever-afters."

Olive sulked. She gave the movie her full attention. Neither of them said anything more about Kayla's dance team or Olive's documentary project. And not one peep about unclear futures and imminent unwanted fates.

Chapter Twenty-Nine

So?

THE MAGIC M&M'S HAD declared impending doom for Mr. Dodd's film-camp endorsement. But Olive chose to listen to Jonáe instead. She blasted their latest hit, "(Shake, Shake, Shake) Shake It Away."

The commission was voting in only three days! Their vote would decide whether to permanently close beaver trapping and hunting on Oregon federal land. So Olive did what she did best. She made more reels.

Sitting in her director's chair, Olive combed through

her latest footage. Leevitt the Beaver at the basketball game and their beaver watching trip at Johnson Creek. She'd even downloaded film from online. The news report about the dead beaver found in her neighborhood and Stumptown Fil at the Oregon Zoo predicting an early spring.

Olive made note of the best shots and started a list of facts she hadn't already shared. Stuff like how beavers building dams and digging canals created fireproof shelters for plants and animals. It even helped slow down the spread of wildfire! And how beaver ponds and wetlands filter out water pollution and support salmon, several which were threatened in Oregon, some even endangered.

Beavers also had transparent eyelids that protect their eyes underwater. But one of Olive's favorite facts is that beavers don't give up! When their dams are destroyed, they rebuild them as quickly as forty-eight hours!

After the success of her previous reels, one posted every day over the past week, Olive was thinking about maybe making a short documentary. Maybe David and Jo would help. Jo could direct. David could do the interviews. Maybe she would even show it to Mr. Dodd and Mr. Summers, and they could help her share it with the community!

Sure, the Magic M&M's had predicted Olive wouldn't get the recommendation. There was always a chance that they were wrong. And if they were right? She wasn't going to let her excitement fizzle out.

Not only could she still make it into Rose City, but Olive didn't want to stop until that ugly law allowing the extermination of beavers was gone.

"I've got ideas!" Olive said, rubbing her palms together.

Jo cocked their eyebrow suspiciously.

Last week in film, the class had focused on getting footage for their documentary projects. They were back in the classroom this week to put their trailers together.

Yesterday, Mr. Dodd had given a lengthy discussion on what makes a good trailer and different editing techniques. They'd also watched a bunch of how-to videos for their After Effects software, from several types of video cuts to adding sound effects and music.

"I watched a lot of trailers last night," Olive said, "and—"

"Ooh!" David squealed. "Which ones?"

With a smile, Jo shook their head.

Olive giggled. "*Girls Rock!, I Am Eleven, The Bully Effect*, and tons more."

"So?" Jo drummed their fingers.

"So," Olive mocked, using the same huffy tone, then warmly smiled, "I paid attention and put together a plan."

She opened up her notebook and ran her finger down the page. "This list is all the footage we've either filmed or downloaded from royalty-free sites."

Olive flipped the page. "And this is how I see it all coming together on the screen.

"It's broken down into scenes." She pointed at the various rows. "The first column shows what the audience will see. Videos, photos, text, transitions, and special effects. The second is what they'll hear. Music, dialogue, voice-overs, and sound effects."

David and Jo grew silent.

Olive tapped her finger on her desk. She waited

impatiently as they began reading over her movie trailer script.

VIDEO	AUDIO
Text: What's Up, Doc! Productions Text Animation: Grow and turn Transition: Fade to black	Natural Sound (7th-grade lunch footage): Echo of students' chatter and laughter and other indistinct sounds.
Special Effect: Fade in Video: 7th-grade lunch footage Special Effect: Blurred background Transition: Jump cut	Music (background): Upbeat, chill Voice-Over (7th-grade lunch footage): "Do you think the Food Fight of 1988 had really happened?" Clips from student interviews sharing different accounts and opinions. Sound Effect: School bell ringing

Olive shifted in her seat. She watched as their eyes slowly moved over the first few lines. Heart pounding, she couldn't take it anymore. Olive exploded with enthusiasm.

"All the teasers are here! Fred's name in the school yearbook, mysterious background music, Mr. Miller saying that Fred was fed up, and a cutaway shot of a can of creamed corn!"

Giddy, Olive trembled. Before her teammates could respond, she kept on gushing.

"But we don't give anything away! We don't reveal that Fred's *not* a redhead by blurring his school photo. And we don't explain why he's fed up."

Olive gripped her desk and leaned forward. "My favorite is the final text and voice-over, which makes the perfect logline—'Sometimes rumors turn out to be mostly true.'"

"Can't you just see the movie poster?"

Olive sat back, arms folded across her chest. She couldn't stop grinning.

David and Jo looked at each other with raised brows.

"Wow!" David beamed.

"I've never heard you talk for so long, and never with this much excitement." Jo nodded with approval. "We got a plan!"

"We got a plan," repeated Olive.

She was finally starting to believe that they had a shot at Mr. Dodd's recommendation! Her confidence was at least 75, 80 percent!

Chapter Thirty

Zombified

FINALLY, THE BIG DAY had arrived! Today the Oregon Fish and Wildlife Commission was making their decision about permanently closing beaver trapping and hunting.

Olive rushed into first period and perched onto her seat next to David.

"Any word?"

His attention on his phone, David shook his head. "Didn't you get Jo's text?"

Olive dug through her backpack. She pulled out her cell and groaned.

"My phone's dead." Once again, she'd forgotten to charge it.

"Jo's dad let them stay home this morning to watch the commission meeting online together," David said, still fixated on his phone. "It's been going on for over an hour, but the petition still hasn't come up yet."

Olive leaned in, peeking at his screen. "Is that the live meeting?"

David nodded. The sound was off, but a transcript of the dialogue typed across the video as people talked. The two watched in silence until the first-period bell rang. As soon as class ended, David whipped out his phone. A text from Jo read: Still nothing.

Olive somehow managed to get through science and social studies, even though she'd barely paid any attention. Annoyed that her phone was dead, she hustled to the common area, hoping to get an update from David before eating lunch.

David and Jo were at her locker. Once Olive caught their troubled faces, her speed slowed to a crawl.

No, no, no, no, no, no, nonononononononono . . .

David hung his head.

Jo balled their hands into fists. "They voted against the petition."

Jo continued talking, their voice seething, but Olive heard nothing.

A heaviness settled over her. It didn't make any sense! The rally had been a huge success: high turnout, press coverage, and loads of people promising to contact the commission. Even her KidVid posts combined had reached over fifty thousand views before today's meeting!

How could they vote no?

The heaviness caved in. She could hardly breathe.

Olive excused herself and bolted to the bathroom. She splashed cold water on her face. She took long, deep breaths. But the weight remained.

"Sorry, Waddle," she whispered to her reflection.

What's the point of speaking up if nothing good comes from it?

Zombified, Olive had no idea how she'd made it through the rest of the day. The worst part was that she needed her best friend. But Kayla had been gone at her doctor's appointment. With her dead battery, Olive couldn't even text her.

One more class to go. And even though film was her favorite, she was dreading it.

Avoiding eye contact with David and Jo, Olive slipped into her seat just as the bell rang. The last thing she wanted to do was talk about the commission's vote against the petition.

"I've been getting some questions about the written plan"—Mr. Dodd tugged on his suspenders—"so let's have a class discussion to address any concerns before we get back to editing in your groups."

Olive tried to pay attention, but her thoughts kept drifting back to Waddle.

I just don't get it.

I say nothing. It doesn't matter.

I say something. It doesn't matter.

Tons of people take action. It still *doesn't matter.*

Jo's brassy tone cut through Olive's fog.

"Olive, are you going or not?"

"Huh?"

"I mentioned it earlier." Jo rolled their eyes. "At the lockers?"

Olive gave a blank look.

Jo released an aggravated sigh. "I know you're frustrated about the vote. We are too. But just because you lose an inning, you don't walk away from the game."

Olive blinked rapidly, not sure what Jo was getting at.

"My dad's taking us to another Busy Beavers volunteer meeting after school. To talk about next steps. It's important that we keep on fighting. Are you coming?"

Why bother? Why pretend we can make a difference?

It's not like they were old enough to make any real change. This was a grown-up problem for grown-ups to fix. But when she caught David's hopeful gaze, Olive hesitated.

She remembered when he'd first seen the cover image of Waddle on her KidVid post. He'd been so excited to share everything he knew about beavers. If it weren't for David, Olive wouldn't have started making reels. Even though the vote hadn't gone their way, she'd finally taken action. Not only for Oregon beavers, but also for Waddle.

That has to mean something. It matters.

Beavers don't give up!

"Count me in," Olive said. "We won't give up!"

Chapter Thirty-One

Where Were You?

ON THE RIDE HOME from the volunteer meeting, Olive's brain was spinning. For once, her thoughts weren't about impending doom. Turns out there were lots of organizations working hard to save beavers—not only in Oregon—but throughout the country.

They'd learned about an Oregon House bill to protect beavers to reduce climate change effects. A public hearing was being held next month where anyone could provide testimony, either in support of or against the bill.

There was also a group of scientists, nonprofits, and advocates from around the country who had sent a letter to the president. The letter urged him to issue an executive order to end beaver trapping and hunting on all US public lands in response to the climate crisis. Two hundred and fifty activists had signed the letter—including the awesome Jonáe! So Busy Beavers had started a petition calling on the president to protect beavers on public land. Now they only needed to get as many signatures as possible.

Mr. Summers's encouraging speech at the volunteer meeting was exactly what Olive had needed to get out of her funk. She bounced in the back seat, excited to share her thoughts.

"We should get other kids involved," Olive blurted.

"Whatcha thinking?" Jo piped from the front seat.

"We could ask the principal to talk about the public hearing in the morning announcements. And we could put a link to the Busy Beavers' petition on the school website," said Olive. "That way students, parents, and teachers can just click a link and sign."

"Great idea, Olive," Mr. Willems said.

Olive beamed. She felt alive again. More people who

knew about the benefits of beavers meant more people would care enough to speak out about it. Which meant a greater chance that the Oregon House bill could become law. And maybe this petition might convince the president of the United States to save *all* beavers!

"Hmmm." Jo said, tapping their chin. "Good but not great."

"Jo," their dad said in that be-nice tone.

Olive frowned.

"Nobody really listens to the morning announcements." Jo waved their hands. "And I doubt most students and parents even look at the school website. David, do you look at the website?"

David shrugged. "At the lunch menu and the game schedule, but that's about it."

"Dad, do you look at the website?"

"No," he said hesitantly.

"My point exactly," Jo said. "But you're onto something, Olive."

Olive wrinkled her nose.

"Maybe," David chimed in, "we could set up a table at school and hand out fliers for kids to take home to their parents or to hang at local businesses."

"Or even better," Jo said, "we could have them sign the petition right then and there! We could also send an email to them or their parents about the public hearing. Imagine if a ton of people showed up in support of the bill and testified. That'll blow their minds!"

Olive bit her lip. She was wary about setting up a table at school and engaging with all the sixth, seventh, *and* eighth graders. Why hadn't she kept her *brilliant* idea to herself.

What would she say if someone asked her a question about beavers that she couldn't answer? Sure, she could share some fun facts, like how some humans have worn smelly beaver goo, but she wasn't an expert like David. She just knew that exterminating beavers was wrong.

Olive shook her head.

None of this is about me. Saving beavers means saving the planet.

Beavers don't give up. So I won't give up.

Once they arrived at her house, Olive jumped out of the car with a rushed good-bye and dashed into the house. She quickly plugged in her phone. Bopping from side to side, she waited for it to come back to life.

After the longest minute ever, Olive pulled up her messages. She ignored the missed texts from Jo and David from before lunch. No need to relive the play-by-play about the denied petition. Not surprisingly, the first conversation on the list with unread texts were from Kayla.

Olive's eyebrows shot up. Her gaze lingered on Kayla's most recently sent message previewed on the screen: WHERE WERE YOU?

Kayla's words—*WHERE WERE YOU?*—pulsed in Olive's head.

Then it hit her. She realized her colossal mistake.

Today Kayla was leading the dance squad at the basketball game. The one with Kayla's signature move. The incredibly important game so the dance team could decide on who would be the replacement cocaptain: Kayla or Abigail.

Olive glanced at the time.

Correction: Kayla had *already* led the team.

Wait! David had been with her and Jo at the volunteer

meeting! If there'd been a game, he wouldn't have gone, right? He'd have been prancing around the court in his Leevitt to Beaver costume.

Slumped on her bed, Olive couldn't avoid it any longer. It didn't matter where David had been.

She clicked on the conversation and read all Kayla's texts that she'd missed since that morning.

Ugh. Can't believe I have that annoying doc appt TODAY ON GAME DAY ALL THE WAY IN SALEM! Mom promises she'll get me back in time but I'm FREAK-ING OUT! Can u tell?

FINALLY in Salem and they're behind!
What if I miss the game?!!
Will Abigail automatically become cocaptain??!!

Meet me before the game at our lockers.
Really freaking out :(

Where are you?
You're still coming tonight, right?

Seriously, are u ok?

WHERE ARE YOU?!!!

WHERE WERE YOU?

Olive cringed. How could she forget? It's the only thing Kayla's been stressing over for almost three weeks. Quickly, she texted: I'M SO SORRY I MISSED IT. PLEASE FORGIVE ME.

No response.

Olive paced her room, reading through Kayla's messages again and again. Still no word.

Feeling dizzy, Olive called Kayla. But it went straight to voicemail.

"Hey!" Kayla's cheery voice said. "When you hear the beep, hang up, and send me a text."

"Hey, it's me. I forgot to charge my phone again, so I just got your texts," Olive tried to explain. "I was so upset when the beaver petition was denied, so I had to go to the Busy Beavers meeting after school, and I don't know how, but I totally forgot about your game. I'm so, so sorry.

"I know it's no excuse. I screwed up. A promise is a promise. I should've been there. But I never meant to hurt you. Besties for life, right?"

Blasting Jonáe's song "Super Villain," Olive fell back onto her bed. She slipped off her glasses and wiped at the tears streaming down her cheeks. Staring at the blurry ceiling, her body shivered.

Maybe if I give Kayla space, then she won't be so mad anymore. Then I can explain it to her in person and she'll understand I would never hurt her on purpose. Then maybe Kayla will forgive me.

Chapter Thirty-Two

I Put a Spell on You

IF ONLY OLIVE HAD a genie's lamp or a monkey's paw. Then she could wish that Kayla would hear her apology, forgive her, and forget all about the terrible mistake that Olive had made. But Olive didn't have some magical genie or paw to grant her three wishes.

All she had was the hope that Kayla had realized that Olive was really sorry.

When Olive stepped onto the school bus, every bit of hope seeped out of her. Kayla sat in their usual spot.

But instead of saving room for Olive, she was giggling with Heather from her dance team.

Olive tried to make eye contact, but Kayla wouldn't look in her direction.

Olive lingered at their lockers before first period. She wasn't even sure what to say that hadn't already been said. Maybe hearing her apology in person would make all the difference. But Kayla never showed.

Later that day, when Olive arrived in Spanish class, Kayla was sitting in a different spot near the front. The only empty chair, a few rows back, was right next to Bobby Filmore!

Olive crumpled into her seat.

During class, Olive eyed the back of Kayla's head, staring intently at her bubble braids. Tapping a finger on both temples, Olive tried sending her best friend mind messages:

I'm sorry I messed up. I'm sorry I missed you leading the dance team. I'm sorry I failed at being your best friend. I'm sorry I'm sorry I'm sorry. . . .

Olive sat at their usual table during lunch. She didn't touch her country fried steak and mashed potatoes with chunky gravy. Her heartbeat picked up every time some-one entered the lunchroom. And then her heart plummeted every time it wasn't Kayla. Her heart crumbled when she realized that Kayla was sitting and laughing with Heather and April from the dance squad.

Later that evening, Olive sat on her bedroom floor. Her phone dinged repeatedly. She glanced at the screen and frowned. Nothing from Kayla.

Ignoring the messages from David and Jo, she silenced her phone. Olive had more important things to do. She was determined to make Kayla forgive her.

They'd been best friends since kindergarten, and Olive wasn't going to let this mistake ruin everything. She might not have that genie or monkey's paw, but magic was still on Olive's side.

Magic was make believe. It was the first and most important rule of magic.

Aunt T had told Kayla and Olive that whatever you believed—no matter if it were fact or fantasy—that belief was made real. To "make" was to bring something into existence. And to "believe" was to accept something as true. Magic only worked if you believed in yourself.

As much as Olive wanted to believe in herself, she often had to fake it. She tried hard to learn control. To make believe it.

Magic—and real life—were a mirror of everything you believed. The good, the bad, and the ugly. So it was important to choose your beliefs wisely.

With over 100 percent confidence, Olive believed that Kayla and her would be best friends forever. Yes, she'd hurt her best friend. But if Kayla would just forgive and forget, then they could move on and go back to how things were. Back to how things should be.

Olive decided to do a "Forgive and Forget" spell.

She lit a strawberry-scented candle to melt Kayla's resistance. She glanced at the time. It was almost six o'clock. Using her mom's old alarm clock, Olive wound the clock backward, slowly turning back time. The hour and minute hands spun past the numbers, passing every hour, until Kayla would've arrived at five thirty last night. A half hour before the basketball game had started.

Olive unwrapped a block of baking chocolate—the 100 percent unsweetened kind—and broke off a square. Holding her nose, she popped the piece into her mouth and chewed. She almost gagged as she forced the gross bitterness down her throat. It represented the hurt and hate Kayla held toward her.

Picking up a fun-sized bag of Skittles, Olive said, "Replace the bitterness with the sweet." She tore it open and picked out the strawberry-flavored pieces, Kayla's favorite, and ate all eight candies at once.

With her eyes closed, Olive sat there for a long time in silence. Many awful thoughts ran through her mind, but she fought them off as best as she could.

I'm a horrible friend.

Must learn control.

Kayla will hate me forever.

Kayla and I are besties for life!

I hate myself. I suck. I'm the worst.

I'll do better from now on.

Olive opened her eyes. "I have been forgiven. The bitterness has been forgotten. The sweetness of our friendship has been restored." Leaning forward, she blew out the candle.

Chapter Thirty-Three

I Ruin Everything

WHEN OFFERED A RIDE to school, it wasn't hard to say yes to Jo. Olive didn't want to face Kayla ignoring her again on the bus. Or watch Kayla having fun with someone that wasn't her.

Olive believed in her "Forgive and Forget" spell. But she didn't have a clue how long it would take to start working. Another rule of magic, it didn't wear a watch. It could take hours, days, even weeks. As frustrating as it was, magic had its own timetable.

Jo's dad dropped Olive, Jo, and David off at school an hour before first period. Their science teacher and the environmental club adviser, Mr. Ference, had agreed to help out. He let them into the building since it was still a half hour before it opened. The three tables Jo had requested were waiting in the commons area, near the lockers.

Jo and David had gotten permission from the administrative office to have up to six students man the tables before school, during each lunch period, and for an hour after school.

Three of David's friends from the environmental club, including Vicky from the Busy Beavers rally, were also there. Jo had already recruited three sixth graders for sixth-grade lunch, four of her eighth-grade friends from her softball team for eighth-grade lunch, and the three of them plus David's friends for seventh-grade lunch and after school.

"You guys made this last night?" Olive asked as she helped drape one of the tables with a brown sheet. Across the front in large block letters were the words: SAVE THE BEAVERS. SAVE THE PLANET.

David nodded. "When you didn't respond to our texts, Jo was going to suggest—"

"You mean 'order.'" Olive laughed.

David cracked up. "Yeah, they were going to require your presence last night, but I reminded them that the world didn't revolve around them. That everyone has a life outside of Jo."

Olive gave a sad smile.

David was right. The world didn't revolve around her either. That was exactly why she was giving Kayla space. But her best friend still wanted nothing to do with her. The growing distance between them was eating her up inside.

Olive glanced at her phone. Still no text. No email. No voicemail.

After the tables were set up, everyone gathered around Jo.

"Everyone should have brought a tablet or phone," Jo said. "I sent an email with two important things. A link to the Busy Beavers website. And an email draft about the upcoming public hearing.

"We want to get as many students as possible to sign the petition asking the president to stop the murdering of all beavers on US public lands. If this executive order happens, it will definitely reduce climate change. Just click on the link so they can sign.

"Then forward the email draft to their parents so they can also sign the petition and help us support the new House bill protecting Oregon beavers. Easy peasy!"

Vicky raised her hand. "What if they ask questions?"

Jo waved their phone. "The email has all the information about the petition plus websites people can go to for more details."

David loudly cleared his throat.

"And we have our resident beaver expert here to answer any questions." Jo smirked.

Everyone chuckled. David wore a smug grin.

David and Vicky stood behind the center table. Olive and Jo manned the table to the right. There were still five minutes until the building opened. Olive nervously bounced on her feet.

Jo made a face. "What's up?"

"Uh, well, have you, um . . ." Olive wrung her hands. "I mean, uh—"

"Spit it out."

"Have you ever, uh . . . gotten into a fight?"

Jo's brows shot up.

"Not hitting and yelling, but . . . like a misunderstanding. With a friend."

"With a name like Mean Vegan Jo, what do you think?"

Olive blushed.

"Kidding!" Jo bumped her shoulder. "Don't tell me you and David are fighting again."

Olive shook her head. "Kayla."

"Yeah." Jo sighed. "Best friends can be tricky."

"I kind of messed up." Olive kept twisting her hands.

"Did you tell her that?"

"Yeah," Olive said. "But she's still mad."

"She probably just needs more time." Jo shrugged. "If she's really your friend, it'll work out."

Before Olive could respond, students began trickling into the school. A few kids approached their table. Jo's voice boomed as they explained what was going on. Olive blew out a series of short breaths. Somehow she managed to get two signatures on the Busy Beavers petition.

Soon the trickle became a flood. Olive's nerves tensed. Just as another student approached, the fairy chimes ringtone chirped on her phone. She beamed once she saw Kayla's name.

"Be right back."

Olive stood off to the side. Her smile vanished.

You ruined everything!

Her face grew warm. She kept starting to respond. But with each unfinished sentence, she tapped the delete key, watching each letter disappear, and started all over again.

Finally, Olive settled on a response and hit send: I don't know how else to say I'm sorry.

What can I do to make things right?

Kayla: It's too late.

Olive sucked in her breath. Too late? But . . . why?

Olive: Did you get my messages?

My phone was dead.

I was upset about the beavers.

I forgot about the game.

It wasn't on purpose.

Kayla: I don't care about your silly beavers!

Catch a hint, Olive Blackwood, and leave me alone.

Olive's head started pounding. Her fingers grazed her temples. Trembling, her breathing grew unsteady.

She felt like her body was moving at the speed of light even though she was still standing still.

Olive was lightheaded, and her mind raced nonstop.

Kayla hates me. What am I going to do? I can't live without my best friend! How could I let her down like that? She would've been there for me. I totally deserve it. I hate me too. Must learn control. Control. Control. Con—

Oh no! I forgot the rules of magic! Spells should never *be used to make someone's choice for them! It's all my fault. I'm the problem. I ruin everything.*

Olive's hand flew to her throat. Gasping, she couldn't breathe. She wanted to run for help. But she was frozen. *I'm dying!*

Lockers stopped slamming. Conversations ceased. She could feel everyone staring at her.

Am I sweating? Am I shaking? Does everyone know what a horrible person I am?

The only sound Olive could hear was her heart thumping in her ears.

Thumpthumpthumpthumpthumpthumpthump.

Her knees buckled and she crumpled to the floor.

Chapter Thirty-Four

Worst Day Ever

A FEW SECONDS OF BLACK.

FADE IN:

INTERIOR CASCADIA MIDDLE
SCHOOL COMMONS. A MINUTE
LATER.

Silence.

CLOSE-UP AND PAN OVER
different pairs of students'
shoes (surrounding Olive).
We hear a heart beating
rapidly. We pull back to
REVEAL Olive is lying on the
floor, surrounded by shocked
students.

FADE IN: Indistinct student
                    chatter.

Jo and David are kneeling
by Olive's side. David is
frightened.

                  JO
   Olive! Olive! Are you okay?

Olive isn't sure if she's
dreaming or not. She tries to
speak but can't. She panics. She

hyperventilates. Her hands fly
to her throat. Olive realizes
that she can't breathe.

ZOOM IN ON OLIVE'S TERRIFIED
FACE. Silence for a few
beats.

    OLIVE'S DAD (VOICE-OVER)
    Olive, baby . . . I'm
    here.
    Breathe for me.

ZOOM IN on Dad's hand holding
Olive's.

          OLIVE
    Dad?

    OLIVE'S DAD (VOICE-OVER)
    Breathe, baby. . . .
    Breathe.

PARAMEDIC (VOICE-OVER)
Olive, take a deep
breath.
I know you're scared. But
I'm with you.
Breathe, Olive. . . .
Breathe.

Olive makes eye contact with
the paramedic. She realizes
the paramedic is holding her
hand. She's crushed that it's
not her dad. The paramedic
calmly demonstrates how to
breathe with exaggerated
inhales and exhales. Olive
slowly mimics the breathing.

FADE IN: "BEST DAY EVER"
by SpongeBob SquarePants,
playing at a slower tempo
and sung instead by the

starfish character, Patrick
Star. Sounds far away.

The paramedic and their
partner help Olive to her
feet. Olive sees a handful
of students staring at her
as they're reluctantly being
guided by teachers to get
to class. Olive winces in
embarrassment. The paramedics
walk Olive down an empty
hall. The late bell rings.
They stop at a closed door.
ZOOM IN on the door plate:
SCHOOL NURSE.

                    CUT TO:

Am I Dying?

OLIVE WAS LIVING HER worst nightmare. First the school watched her fall out and almost die. Then the paramedics. Now this. Stuck in the nurse's office. She hated doctors.

She sat on the examination table, her legs hanging over the edge. She couldn't stop squirming. With every move that Olive made, the annoying white paper crinkled.

Even though Olive had already gone through this

with the paramedics, Mrs. Halloway checked Olive's temperature, blood pressure, and heart rate. After each result the school nurse mumbled to herself, "Uh-huh," and entered notes on her tablet. She moved on to examining Olive's ears, eyes, and throat.

When Mrs. Halloway seemed to be done with all her tests, Olive anxiously waited to find out if she'd passed.

"I called your mother, and she should be here soon, but if you have any—"

A teacher Olive didn't recognize bolted inside. "Mrs. Halloway! You're needed in the gym right away!"

The nurse handed Olive a bottle of water. "Just rest and relax. I'll be right back."

My best friend dumped me. Everyone saw my freak-out. The paramedics came.

And I'm supposed to relax?

Olive covered her face with her palms.

Was Kayla there? Was Abigail with her? Were they laughing at me?

Was Kayla wondering why she was ever friends with such an oddball?

Olive felt like she was dying all over again.

She let out a shaky exhale. It was claustrophobic in the small room. There were no windows. The harsh overhead fluorescent lights buzzed. Olive wrinkled her nose. It smelled sharp and musty, like rubbing alcohol, with a hint of sour.

Olive sipped on the water. She hadn't realized how dry her mouth was. Rolling the bottle cap in her hand, she took in all the colorful posters covering the walls. There was a My Plate chart. Several human-body posters, including the muscular, skeletal, and nervous systems.

Olive's gaze lingered on the poster with a fat orange cat, his teeth clenched and tail puffed up. The title read: CATASTROPHIC SIGNS OF ANXIETY. Squiggly written words—*fear, muscle tension, fatigue, racing heart, antsy, stomach problems*—crowded in and around the cat.

Underneath were other illustrations: the cat relaxing; a thought bubble over the cat's head showing anxiety triggers; and the cat hugging a cartoon mouse, sharing his fears.

Olive's stomach flipped.

Is that what's happening to me?

The door creaked open. Mrs. Halloway returned, but she wasn't alone. Ms. Grant, the school counselor, stood by her side.

Olive froze.

"Sorry about that," Mrs. Halloway said. "I brought Ms. Grant, in case you want to talk about what happened."

"We can talk about anything you want, Olive." Ms. Grant gave a warm smile. "I'm here for you."

Olive glanced at the CATastrophic Signs of Anxiety poster and blurted, "Am I dying?"

"Oh, honey, no," said Ms. Grant. "The paramedics said you had a panic attack."

Olive's eyes widened.

Panic? Attack? In front of the entire school?

There was no way she was going to class now. Everyone must be laughing about her. The girl and her freak attack.

Had Kayla told everyone why? That I'm the worst friend in the entire world?

Olive patted her jean pockets. Her heart raced. They were both empty.

"Here you go, hon." Mrs. Halloway handed Olive her phone.

Olive's face overheated. Had the nurse read her texts? Had she shared it with the school counselor? Was that why they were both staring at her like she was some kind of weirdo?

"Your friend, Jo, picked it up for you," Mrs. Halloway said.

Olive wondered if her embarrassing story would be passed down through history, like the Food Fight of 1988. The Panic Attack. Olive would become a legend in the worst possible way. Her mind raced with all the possible versions, including being expelled for causing a scene, falling into a coma, and being unable to breathe and suffocating to death.

"Do you have any questions?" Ms. Grant asked.

Olive's pulse quickened. She had lots of questions. But the one that mattered most, the counselor couldn't answer.

Will Kayla ever forgive me?

Mom squeezed Olive so tight, she could hardly breathe.

"Oh, honey." Her voice was shaky. "Are you okay? I

was so worried. When they called and said . . . I just, I can't, are you okay?"

Standing in the middle of the nurse's office, Olive tried to relax into Mom's arms. She couldn't believe how quickly she'd arrived. So often Mom didn't even make it home before dinner.

Olive wanted to tell her everything. She wanted Mom to say that everything was going to be okay. But how could she with an audience? The nurse and counselor were still there.

Olive pulled away.

"Sorry to make you miss work," she mumbled. "I know how important it is."

Mom frowned. "You are always more important than work."

Ms. Grant cleared her throat. "Why don't we go to my office for a minute, Mrs. Blackwood, and then you can take Olive home?"

"I'll be right back, sweetie." Mom squeezed Olive's hand.

All three women left, leaving Olive alone. Somehow the room felt even smaller.

Olive paced, not knowing where to look or what to do. So, as usual, her thoughts took over.

Panic attack. I had a panic attack! Does this mean I'm losing it?

Olive hugged her chest.

I wanna go home. I hate doctors. I hate waiting. I—

Suddenly, Olive remembered another time she'd been waiting for her mom.

It had been a long time ago, back when she was in the first grade. Usually, Dad had picked her up from school, but he'd had a doctor's appointment. His cancer had been getting worse. So he'd been spending more time at the hospital. Mom had been busy at work and forgot to pick Olive up. Her parents had spent all night fighting. Then a month or so later, Dad had died.

Olive's heart raced.

Control, Olive Blackwood. Must learn control.

It felt like an eternity, but finally the office door opened. Mom returned alone. She hugged Olive again, but this time Olive didn't hug her back.

"I'm sorry I didn't realize that something was wrong," Mom said. "I should've noticed. Does this have something to do with that conversation we had a few weeks ago? The one about the wildfires? And beavers?"

Olive swallowed hard. Mom's face was worried and sad and somehow hopeful all at the same time. Even with the nurse and counselor gone. Even with the strong urge to share everything, Olive just nodded.

"The counselor suggested it might help for you to talk with a therapist."

Olive grew stiff.

"I think it's a good idea. I was able to get an appointment on Tuesday. Our doctor says that Dr. Green is excellent."

"I don't want to go to a therapist," Olive huffed.

"It's not up for discussion," she said firmly. "You're going."

Mom's face softened. She handed Olive a thin book with a light blue cover. The title read: *Quiet Your Anxiety.*

"This isn't an official diagnosis, but we think you're dealing with some frightening thoughts and feelings that caused your panic attack. Maybe looking at this before Tuesday could help put you at ease."

Mom's hopeful eyes weighed heavy on her.

Olive shrugged.

Mom let out a heavy sigh. She tucked a lock of curls behind Olive's ear and looked her directly in the eye. "Honey, your feelings are valid, but that doesn't make them a fact."

Olive's shoulders relaxed a teeny bit.

"Let's go home."

Thankfully, classes were still in session. The halls were empty and eerily quiet.

Once they got to the car, Olive checked her phone. There were unread texts in her conversation with David and Jo. But nothing from Kayla.

Olive finally got the message. They were no longer friends.

Chapter Thirty-Six

Never Going Back

OLIVE SILENTLY READ THE title of the book the nurse had given her mom, *Quiet Your Anxiety*.

She flipped through the pages. Some were covered with lots of text—the words *anxiety*, *fear*, *stress*, and *worry*—popping up in bold repeatedly. Others had a writing prompt at the top and blank lines for journaling a response.

Olive snorted. Even back at home in the safety of her bedroom, there was nothing that could silence her paralyzing thoughts. Especially not some book. It was so thin. There's no way it could hold all the fears that filled her with dread. She tossed the book aside.

There was a knock at Olive's door. She slid back on her bed, pulling her knees into her chest. "Come in."

Mom poked in her head. "Hungry?"

Olive shook her head.

Mom's lips contorted, as if she were struggling with what to say. She tiptoed inside, stopping short of Olive's bed. Olive was starting to feel radioactive. As if no one wanted anything to do with her, otherwise they might get burned.

Silence.

It was that same awkwardness shared during the car ride home.

Mom perched on the corner. "I want to give you some space, but . . ."

Olive shivered. That word again. "Space."

"But I hope you know I'm always here for you. For anything."

Nodding, Olive didn't make eye contact.

"And even though you're seeing Dr. Green on Tuesday,

we can talk more about the wildfires and beavers and anything else, if you want, after you've rested."

Olive managed a small smile but said nothing.

After Mom closed the door behind her, Olive pulled out her phone. Still no message from Kayla. She clicked on the unread conversation with Jo and David.

Jo: Are you okay?

David: We missed you in film class. Don't worry, we turned in the written plan.

Jo: A simple thumbs-up is all we need to know you're okay.

David: Reach out whenever you're ready.

Olive felt a flush creep over her cheeks. How could she ever show her face at school again? There's no way she could go to the school assembly now and present their documentary trailer! Her throat tightened as she imagined everyone—students, teachers, and parents—staring at her. What if she had another panic attack?

She hit the thumbs-up emoji on Jo's message and typed Sorry, but I'm not going to the assembly on Thursday. Sorry. She quickly turned off her phone and tossed it to the end of her bed. It landed on top of the thin blue book, covering the title, *Quiet Your Anxiety*.

It didn't matter whether her thoughts were fact or fiction. The tense shoulders, shallow breath, and pounding heart, were all real.

Olive was never leaving her room again.

Olive spent the weekend lying in bed watching fantasy movies. She didn't want Monday, and especially not Tuesday, to come.

Mom had often checked in on her. She'd even cooked dinner and they'd sat down at the dining room table on Saturday *and* Sunday evening. Though Olive appreciated the gesture, most of the time was spent in uncomfortable silence.

A few times Olive had considered picking up the *Quiet Your Anxiety* journal. But the thought would fly by quick. It was bad enough that she was being forced to see some therapist.

Why relive those jumpy, paralyzing feelings again? Uh-uh. No way. No thank you.

Not once had Olive turned on or even touched her phone and she had completely avoided email and

KidVid. But she'd spent a lot of time in her head.

Sunday night while watching the Swamp of Sorrow scene in *The NeverEnding Story*, her daydreaming turned dark. She imagined that instead of Atreyu struggling to save his drowning horse, it was Kayla standing over Olive as she slowly sunk into the muddy waters. Kayla stared blankly at Olive's outstretched hand.

Those awful words rang in her head: *You ruined everything! Catch a hint, Olive Blackwood, and leave me alone.*

Olive picked at her lips. She recalled the CATastrophic Signs of Anxiety poster in Mrs. Halloway's office. She followed the poster's advice and breathed deep and slow. She tried reminding herself that right now she was safe in her bed. But she couldn't quiet her mind. Her feelings were too real.

I'm horrible. I'm awful. I'm forever alone.

Olive dug her nails into her palms as the thoughts continued to intrude.

I'm a loser. Forever. Alone.

Monday morning, a knock at her door startled Olive awake. Before she could respond, Mom popped in.

"Morning, sweetie. Just wanted to let you know I'm working from home today."

Olive peeked from under the covers.

"So if you need anything, anything at all, let me know."

Olive nodded.

"I know you're going through a hard time, but why not go for a walk?"

Olive grimaced.

"Or maybe visit Kayla after school?"

Olive stiffened.

"You can't stay in the house forever," Mom said. "At some point, you have to face the world again."

She wanted to argue those statements but sucked in her lips instead.

"I know you're going through a lot, but . . ." Mom stared intently at her manicured nails. "I know what it's like to feel anxious."

Olive furrowed her brow. Mom? Anxious? Yeah, right.

"The first time I did a mock trial in law school, I was *so* nauseous. It was nerve-racking, and I failed horribly." Mom shifted on her feet. "But I did it."

Olive couldn't believe it. Mom looked so small. She'd never seen her insecure before.

"Even now, before I speak in court, I get nervous." Mom hugged her middle. "But I just remind myself *why* I do what I do. I want to help families get through difficult situations."

Olive's lips parted, but still she said nothing.

What could she say? "Good for you, Mom. So glad you're able to face your fears. But me? My anxiety causes poop and panic attacks! Can you still relate?"

"Well . . . you know where to find me." Mom closed the door behind her.

Olive slithered out from under the covers. She wandered over to her desk and picked up her phone. She stared at the black screen and took in a long, slow inhale.

Holding her breath, she pushed in the power button until a photo filled the screen. It was Kayla and her dressed up in their witch costumes at the Halloween dance. Kayla as Glinda the Good, Olive as Evillene.

Olive's heart sunk. It was Monday, February 14. Valentine's Day. V-Day. Doomsday.

She wondered if Kayla had heard back from Jeff. If he'd said yes to her dance invite.

Olive slumped onto her bed. Had Bobby heard about her panic attack? Had he seen it? Was he going to the dance?

She wondered what it would be like to go with a group of friends. And for a moment, she pictured herself with Bobby and Kayla in that group. Not like she'd ever ask him to go. Not like she had any friends to go with. Everyone probably thought she was a total weirdo now. Including Kayla.

Olive needed to talk to someone. But she couldn't imagine sharing all her recent scary moments and paralyzing fears with Mom. Kayla wanted nothing to do with her. And even though she had that therapy appointment tomorrow, she didn't want to talk about it with a total stranger.

Olive just couldn't shake the feeling that she was doomed and alone.

Lucky Charms

"HEY, DAD. I HAD a panic attack." Holding her phone, Olive couldn't face herself on the screen. "It was as scary as it sounds. But I totally deserved it."

Even though her stomach was twisted up in knots, Dad was the only person she felt comfortable talking to. And he was the only person whose thoughts about her would never change. No matter what Olive said to him, he'd always love her and be proud of her, because he knew nothing about the Olive of today.

"Remember how I told you that it's okay to extermi-nate beavers? Well, my friends David and Jo, the ones from my film project team, we've been doing all these things to make that ugly law go away. I was so wrapped up in it that I let Kayla down."

Once she started, Olive couldn't stop. She talked about all the KidVid posts and all the awesome stuff they'd done to help beavers. Then she explained how she'd messed up with Kayla.

"When I got her text to leave her alone, I panicked. What am I going to do without my best friend?

"Mom's always busy with work. You're gone. And now Kayla's left me too."

Olive stopped recording. Her stomach unknotted just a little.

Phone in hand, she went to the kitchen. She loaded a large bowl with Lucky Charms. Olive set the bowl aside, waiting for the marshmallows to start melting into the milk. She loved how they made the milk colorful, sweet, and magically delicious. But what Olive loved best was that each marshmallow charm gave Lucky the lepre-chaun different powers.

Pink hearts brought objects to life, like making his spoon tell corny jokes. Lucky could fly on his shooting stars or run fast thanks to his horseshoes. Clovers brought him luck, and blue moons made him invisible. Unicorns painted his world in vibrant colors. Lucky could teleport using rainbows. And red balloons made him light enough to float.

Olive wished she had a blue moon. Then she could disappear and never go back to school.

Olive and Kayla had read about the marshmallow charm powers online in the fourth grade. That's when they'd decided to make their own magical charm bracelets.

Braiding together three different colors of thread, they'd each added various beads and a unique charm before fastening their bracelets with a knot at the end. Kayla had added a ballet slipper, Olive an R2-D2 charm.

Then came the most important part. They'd whispered their wish to their charm to activate its magical power. Kayla had asked to do well at her dance recitals. And Olive had wished to see her dad again. One month later, she'd received her first video from Dad!

Suddenly, her phone dinged. Olive checked her email. There *was* one good thing about Valentine's Day. Dad's scheduled monthly video message.

"Hey, baby girl," he said with a big grin. "Have I ever told you about my debut film?"

Even though he couldn't see her, Olive shook her head.

"The premiere showing was at the Cal U student union and . . ." His head hung down and after a brief pause, he finished, "It bombed."

Olive's eyes widened.

"I don't like to talk about it because it's not something I like to remember. I wasn't even going to tell you, but . . ." Dad picked at his slightly overgrown beard. "I think it's important for you to know that life isn't always easy. The things you love and want to be great at, you have to keep working at it. Even when it gets hard. Even when it's not fun.

"Not only did some people in the audience boo when the screening was done, but the school newspaper wrote up a harsh review." His usually friendly eyes were sullen. "Even though I kept on filming, it was a long time before I shared my stuff with anyone. Including Mom."

Olive swirled her cereal with her spoon and took a hefty bite. She couldn't believe it. Dad wasn't always 100 percent confident! He'd been afraid of what other people had thought about him and his films. Just like how Jo was afraid of the dark. And how Kayla had been afraid that she wouldn't make cocaptain. Her dad had gotten scared too.

Dad talked about how he'd started submitting other films into contests and festivals, and how he eventually became okay with the unknown.

"I had to be good with what I made and let go of what other people thought about it. Did it hurt when others hated my work? You bet. But I never let it stop me from doing what I loved. What matters is that I do the best I can, whatever that means in each moment."

Olive took off her glasses and rubbed her eyes.

I don't want what other people think about me to stop me from doing what I love. I'm going to the assembly.

It would be scary to speak in front of all those people, with all of them staring her down. But she didn't want to let her teammates—her friends—down. Olive wasn't alone. With David and Jo by her side, she would survive. They would be her lucky charms.

Olive: Hey.

David: Hey!

Jo: HEY! How you doin?

We were worried about you!

Everything ok? Need anything?

Olive: LOL

Thought y'all would be upset with me

David: Of course not!

Jo: Heck no!

Olive: I'm REALLY sorry I bailed, but

I want to go to the assembly

To help present our trailer

If you still want that

Jo: 100%!

David: Wouldn't be the same without you :)

Olive: Thanks, guys!

I won't let you down!

Jo: You're never gonna believe what we found out

Remember the new House bill protecting Oregon beavers?

One of the House reps is gonna be at the assembly!

Olive slapped her palms on the kitchen table. She couldn't believe it!

Turned out, Vicky from David's environmental club was that House representative's daughter! She was also in the cooking club. Since they'd be providing refreshments, her mom, Mrs. Goldmann, was also going to be there to support her.

Jo: David's gonna have Vicky introduce us to her mother.

Then we can tell her why she MUST pass the new bill.

Olive: Gonna do what u do best, David?

Work your magic mascot moves?

Jo: Shake your beaver tail?

David: Ha. Ha.

Olive giggled. She got up from the kitchen table and dumped her bowl in the dishwasher. Not only was she starting to feel better, but she was excited for the assembly!

Sure, her stomach still flip-flopped when she thought about speaking in front of an audience. But now that they had the perfect opportunity to grab the attention of someone who could affect *real* change for the Oregon beavers, how could she not be excited?

Olive's phone pinged. She clicked on the unread message and gasped. It was a text from Kayla.

Can we talk?

Please?

Chapter Thirty-Eight

Tell Me About Yourself

OLIVE LEANED AGAINST THE kitchen island, reading Kayla's message over and over: Can we talk? Please?

Her chest grew warm. Olive had been waiting for days to have a real conversation with Kayla. But now that she'd finally reached out, Olive didn't know how to respond.

No, that wasn't true. Olive was afraid of what Kayla would say.

Every time she started typing a response, she ended up deleting it.

YES, PLEASE!— Delete.

I'm sorry I ruined everything— Delete.

Is it too late to say I'm sorry— Delete.

I care about you and you making cocaptain— Delete.

I never meant to hurt you, do you— Delete.

Do you still hate me?— Delete.

Olive turned off her phone. She just couldn't deal. No matter what she said, the fear was too overwhelming. She wasn't ready for Kayla's response. Especially not after their last text exchange. Just thinking about it made Olive's heart race.

Olive returned to her bedroom and grabbed her tablet. She hid under the covers and escaped into another fantasy movie.

The next day was Olive's first therapy appointment.

Dr. Green was an old man with no hair on his head or face, which was pretty weird for Portland. He was dressed up all businesslike, but without a tie.

Olive rested her hand on her phone in her pocket. Even though it was still turned off since yesterday, just having it brought her some comfort.

"So, Olive," Dr. Green said, "why don't you tell me about yourself?"

Olive looked at the file in his hands. They'd arrived a half hour before her morning appointment so Mom could fill out paperwork. Olive had taken a peek while Mom had scribbled away. She'd answered questions about Olive like age, medical history, and family history. Didn't he have all the answers right in front of him?

Though her stomach fluttered, Olive felt safe. Maybe it was his kind eyes or his soothing deep voice. Or maybe it was because he kind of resembled her dad, if Dad were older and bald.

"What do you want to know?"

Dr. Green chuckled. "Absolutely anything you'd like to share."

Olive considered her options. Sure, she could talk about her panic attack and revisit one of the most horrific moments of her life. That's why she was here, right? And, of course, she could explain what had happened with Kayla that had led to that moment. But Olive decided that if she was going to be somewhere she didn't want to be, and was told to share something that she wanted to talk about, then that's exactly what she'd do.

"Did you know that it's legal to 'take'—aka exterminate—beavers right here in the Beaver State? Pretty messed up, right?"

Dr. Green leaned forward, his face both surprised and amused. "I did not. Tell me more."

Olive launched into a detailed conversation about all the amazing facts she'd been learning, the KidVid posts, and how her, David, and Jo were working hard to save beavers.

"We're activists. Not just for beavers, but to help save the planet."

Olive spilled about seeing Waddle in the park, the beaver chase, and how scary the wildfires were two years ago. She even shared that she hoped she would never be that close to suffocating smoke again.

Dr. Green leaned back in his chair and smiled. Not quite like one of Dad's big toothy grins, but just as warm. "I'm sorry to say that our time is up. But I loved learning about things you really care about. And I look forward to hearing more at our next visit."

Olive jumped to her feet.

"It was a pleasure to meet you, Olive Blackwood." Dr. Green stood up and firmly shook her hand. "Would you have your mom come in while you wait outside?"

Olive nodded.

As she sat alone in the small waiting area, Olive puffed out her chest. She couldn't believe that she'd talked non-stop for almost an hour with a complete stranger! She was also proud of all the stuff that David, Jo, and she had done and all the things they would do. Like convincing the House representative at the assembly to protect Oregon beavers.

Olive realized that she hadn't mentioned anything about her dream of becoming an award-winning director of fantasy movies. Surprisingly, she was okay. The more she thought about it, she wasn't even sure that it was ever her dream to begin with.

Smiling to herself, Olive knew she'd always be involved in filmmaking, one way or another. The possibilities were endless.

Chapter Thirty-Nine

Really Your Friend

IT WAS EIGHT O'CLOCK and Olive still hadn't replied to Kayla's text. She couldn't avoid it any longer. Sitting on her bed, Olive turned on her phone. It chirped. Confused, Olive frowned. There was a video message from Jo.

"Hey, I'm glad you're coming back to school tomorrow." Jo's round face looked full of worry. "And I . . . I debated whether to say anything or not, but—"

Olive's brows raised. Jo, afraid to speak their mind? This couldn't be good.

"I picked up your phone on Friday when, you know"—Jo waved their hands—"and I saw Kayla's texts."

Olive inhaled sharply. *Jo knows?!*

"It's just, you'd said that y'all were fighting and that you'd apologized. And, well, it's none of my business, but . . . what she said, it was pretty harsh."

A flush crept up Olive's cheeks.

Jo's gaze darted downward. "We haven't known each other long, but . . . I know you."

Jo looked back directly into the camera. It was as if Jo were staring right at her.

"You're shy but nice, so whatever you did . . . I doubt you deserved that. Are you sure she's really your friend?"

Olive's eyes widened.

"So, I wanted you to know that I'm here if you need to, you know, talk or whatever. Later."

Olive's chest grew warm. Jo *was* her friend. Was Kayla?

Olive pulled up Kayla's text. She nervously rubbed her arm. Still not ready to respond, Olive hit the record button.

"Hey, Dad." Her voice was soft but steady. "Kayla

finally reached out. She wants to talk, but . . . I don't know what to do. We've been best friends forever. And yeah, we've fought, *a lot*, but we've always made up and moved on. This time feels . . . different."

Olive paused, thinking about Jo's message.

"Sure, I screwed up, but I apologized . . . again and again. What else does she want from me? I didn't mean to hurt her, but what she said . . ."

Olive bit down on her lip. This time she wasn't so much as hurt as she was angry.

"I don't know what's going to happen, but it's time to talk and move on. Together . . . or not."

Olive stopped recording and slid off her bed. The *Quiet Your Anxiety* journal caught her attention. She picked it up off the floor and slowly started flipping through it. She took in the bolded headers: *Mood Tracker, Gratitude, I Felt, Goals, Positive Thoughts* . . .

Olive paused, lingering on the words *Cool Stuff I Want to Do.*

She still wasn't sure how she felt about journaling. Writing down her mood, thoughts, and worries, the idea only brought on more panic. Now that she'd be seeing

Dr. Green every Tuesday after school for the next couple of months, she didn't need this anymore. The more she thought about it, Olive realized that she liked talking to him. It was kind of like filming messages to her dad.

Olive set the book face down on her desk. She was tired of being afraid. She was tired of feeling hurt. There was lots of cool stuff she was ready to do. But there was something she needed to do first.

She brought up Kayla's text and replied.

Let's talk.

Tomorrow morning.

Before school.

In the commons.

Chapter Forty

Worth the Risk

AN EMPTY FEELING SAT heavy inside as Olive waited for Kayla. Surrounded by lockers slamming shut and rowdy chatter, the noise was deafening. So far, her rapid heartbeat and rattled nerves hadn't caused her to implode.

Thankfully, Mom had dropped her off. Olive hadn't wanted to be trapped with Kayla on the bus ride to school. Especially if the conversation got ugly. At least in the commons, Olive could get away. That was if her body didn't freeze again.

It was Olive's first day back since the infamous panic attack. School hadn't even started yet, and already she'd gotten lots of stares. Surprisingly, most seemed worried or saddened, instead of making fun like Olive had anticipated. Still, the attention made her feel itchy and restless.

Control, control, control.

Once she spotted Kayla heading in her direction, Olive grew nauseous. She eyed the nearest exit. Unfortunately, it was too late to escape.

"Hey," Kayla said.

Olive flinched at her gruff voice. Her gaze remained steady on Kayla's feet. She was wearing new sparkly sneakers.

Did Abigail, Heather, or some other dance team member go shopping with her? Is that why she wanted to talk? To tell me we're no longer besties for life?

Even though they were surrounded by bustling activity, all Olive could hear was the silence between them. She cleared her throat. "Hey."

"Thanks for coming." Kayla's usual energetic tone fell flat.

Olive gripped her backpack strap. She made eye contact. Kayla's head turned away. Olive's heart dropped.

Is Kayla really my friend?

"I'm sorry," Olive squeaked. She took a deep breath and let it all spill out.

"I'm sorry I missed you leading the dance team. I should've been there. I wanted to. But I forgot and I feel sick about it. I hope you'll forgive me, but . . ."

Olive swallowed hard, her heart pounding.

"But what you said," Olive continued, "that you didn't care and to leave you alone. That *really* hurt. It . . . it still does."

"I . . ." Kayla's face saddened.

Olive noticed that Kayla's usually styled do was a messy bun. And not the good kind. It was a hot mess.

"I'm really sorry too." Kayla's voice cracked.

Olive's chest warmed.

"When you weren't at the game last week, I was devastated. And . . ." Kayla rubbed her arm hanging limp by her side. "After the game, I was so sure that I'd lost the chance at being cocaptain. I guess I took it out on you."

Kayla explained everything. Abigail had complained

to the cocaptains that Kayla and Olive had plotted against her. That they'd tried to mess up her turn when she'd led the team.

Olive's eyebrows shot up. "Are you kidding me?"

"I wish." Kayla frowned. "Remember when you and Jo were yelling my name?"

Still confused, Olive nodded.

"Abigail said that your 'screeching,'" Kayla said, using air quotes with shiny nails, "had knocked her off her game, so the cocaptains asked me about it. It felt like being interrogated. I told them that we'd never sabotage a fellow teammate, but I was so afraid they wouldn't believe me and would kick me off the team.

"It wasn't fair to take it out on you. When I heard about your panic thing and the ambulance showing up and then when you didn't come back to school, I . . ." She wrung her hands.

"I was so scared. Scared that all those awful things I'd said, that it was all my fault. Scared that you hated me and that you'd never forgive me. I—I didn't know what to do. I was so wrong. I'm sorry I hurt you. Forgive me?"

Olive wrapped Kayla in a bear hug.

Abigail making up a ridiculous tale? Real shocker. At least now Olive understood why Kayla had lashed out at her. She was also proud of standing up for herself.

Kayla gave her a sheepish look.

"Never in a bazillion years could I ever hate you." Olive punched Kayla in the shoulder.

"Ow." Kayla joked. She grabbed her arm and pouted as if in pain.

Olive went to playfully punch her again but said, "Who's the new cocaptain?"

Kayla wiggled her brows.

"I knew it!" Olive jumped up and down. "The Sacred Skittles never lie."

"Yeah, but it's definitely weird now. Especially since Abigail acts as if she's done nothing wrong."

"Forget Abigail," Olive said. "You're cocaptain!"

Kayla laughed. "I'm just glad things are all good with us again!"

Olive held out her pinkie.

Kayla intertwined her finger around Olive's and said, "Besties for life."

• • • • •

"So what's the big emergency?" said Jo.

Olive, David, and Jo stood near the cafeteria entrance. Olive had texted earlier, asking them to meet her at lunch. It was the second time today Olive was in the commons, determined to face her fears.

"I've been thinking about the conversation we're going to have with Vicky's mom. To convince her to vote for the new bill protecting beavers."

"And?" Jo asked.

"Well, even if Mrs. Goldmann listens to us"—Olive picked at her cuticles—"do you think she'll really care about what three seventh graders think?"

"Vicky's in seventh grade, and I'm sure she cares what her daughter thinks, so . . ." David shrugged.

Jo crossed their arms. "Our voices matter as much as anyone's."

"Yeah, but," Olive said, "she probably hears people pleading about their causes all the time. Maybe if we showed her *why* it was important for humans and beavers to live together in harmony, then she might take us more seriously."

David cocked his head curiously.

"What are you getting at?" asked Jo.

"You know my KidVid reels about beavers," Olive said. "Why not present a similar reel at the assembly—*instead* of our food-fight trailer?"

David's eyes bulged. Jo's mouth hung open.

Kayla had said that you'll never know what could happen if you don't speak up. And Olive wanted to keep doing cool stuff, like fighting to save beavers and the planet and making films. She may not be the best with words, but she was good at making reels.

"We can still talk with her," Olive continued, "but we can say so much more with a film. Not only would we reach a House rep, but also every student and teacher at school!"

Olive shifted her weight. "If we do it, we probably won't get the recommendation for Rose City."

"Making films is cool and all," Jo said, "but it's not how I plan on spending my summer."

"I took film because it sounded like fun—and it is—but . . ." David grinned sheepishly. "I'll be going to mascot camp."

"Sweet." Jo shoulder bumped David.

"Well, we may fail the assignment," Olive said, fighting not to fidget. "But I still think it's worth it. But if you don't want to, I understand."

"I think it's a great idea," Jo said. "I'm game."

David grinned. "Let's do it!"

Olive bounced on the balls of her feet. "Thanks, guys! I'll make the film tonight and . . ." She began to frown. "The only thing is, I'm not sure how to submit our fake trailer."

All documentary projects—both the trailer and the written report—had to be uploaded to Mr. Dodd's teacher webpage by tonight, the night before the event. It grew quiet, except for the muffled lunchroom sounds seeping through the door. Olive hugged her stomach. Maybe this wasn't such a great idea after all.

"I got it!" David held up a finger. "We could misspell our title. Something not so obvious. Mr. Dodd would surely allow us to submit a revised file tomorrow!"

"Perfect!" Jo gave David a high five. "He'll never know what's up until it's on the big screen!"

Giddy, Olive couldn't wait!

Chapter Forty-One

Speak To Me

"WHOA," JO SAID, THEIR head swinging back and forth. The school auditorium was packed. "I don't think I've ever seen this many people in here before!"

Olive's heart was beating so hard, her chest was about to burst. She wasn't even sure what was making her the most anxious. Speaking in front of at least two hundred students, teachers, and parents. People recognizing her as the girl who had had the Panic Attack. Or showing her Save the Beavers reel instead of the documentary trailer.

Olive stood in the back with Kayla, David, and Jo. David's and Jo's parents had already wished them luck and retired to the balcony. She tugged on the skirt of her itchy dress that she'd borrowed from Kayla, scanning the crowd. Mom had said she'd try to sneak away from work in time for their trailer. But Olive didn't see her mom anywhere.

"I can't believe we have to go last," Jo scowled.

"You know what they say," David said. "Save the best. . . . Forget the rest."

Jo and Kayla chuckled.

Olive, however, fidgeted with the end of her sweater. She'd feel so guilty if they ended up with a big fat F. Or what if the House rep wasn't there—or, even worse, hated their reel? What if David and Jo never spoke to her again?

Olive dug her nails into her palms.

Control, Olive Blackwood. Must learn control.

She reminded herself that it didn't matter what others thought about her film. Yes, it would hurt if it didn't help save the beavers. But it would hurt more if she didn't take action.

Opening and closing her fists, Olive tried to make believe Dad's advice—

I'm proud that we're showing my film. It doesn't matter what others think.

—but her anxious thoughts kept winning.

My reel is garbage. I'm no expert on beavers. Everyone's gonna laugh. Our team's gonna fail. What was I thinking? Just when everything is good, here I go, messing life up again. When will—

"We should grab seats," Jo said, and headed down the aisle. David followed.

Kayla grabbed Olive's hand and squeezed. "Are you okay?"

Olive snatched her hand away. "I'll be back."

She hustled out of the auditorium and shoved her way to the bathroom. A mother was helping her young kid wash their hands. Next to them, two students were giggling and putting on lip gloss.

Olive's stomach churned. She considered leaving, but there was nowhere else to go. The school was locked. She was trapped. Her cramps worsening, she locked herself in the farthest stall.

Her head buzzed. She wished she could teleport to anywhere in the world. Or into the future. So she wouldn't have to go through with the assembly.

Olive thought she heard the bathroom door open and shut. She strained to hear if anyone was still there. But it didn't matter. It was too late. She'd had her third diarrhea attack at school.

Holding her head in her hands, she was pummeled with catastrophic thoughts.

Why, why, why, I can't go out there now but I can't hide in here forever, can I? I'm so gross. I don't know what to do. I just wanna die why why why please I can't—

"Olive?" a familiar voice called.

Olive startled. She wasn't sure whether to be mortified or relieved.

"It's about to start," Kayla said softly.

"I—I can't go." Olive sniffed back tears.

"It's okay. There's nobody here. It's just me."

Sweating, Olive crept out of the stall. She headed straight to the sink. She washed her hands and splashed cold water on her face.

"I know you're scared," Kayla said, "but you can do this."

Shaking, Olive turned toward Kayla. Her gaze remained on her dress shoes.

"Jo and David will be onstage with you," Kayla said. "And I'll be in the audience. Only look at me. Just speak to me."

Olive slowly made eye contact. Kayla held out her pinkie finger.

Warmth spread across Olive's chest. She intertwined her finger around Kayla's. Her shoulders relaxed and they both smiled.

Chapter Forty-Two

Lights, Camera, Activist!

THE HOUSELIGHTS DIMMED. OLIVE kept breathing, slow and deep. Kayla took Olive's hand and squeezed. Olive squeezed back.

Mr. Dodd walked onto the stage and the room filled with hoots, hollers, and applause. Tonight, his hair was especially messy. He wore a white bow tie and matching suspenders. Olive's eyes widened. It was the first time she'd seen the combo without a cheesy print. Instead, his button-down shirt was covered in little top hats!

"What stops a lunchroom food fight?" Mr. Dodd cupped his ear and leaned toward the crowd, as if expecting a reply. "A peas treaty!"

Groans erupted, but it didn't stop Mr. Dodd from his bad-dad-jokes routine.

"What do you call a fake noodle? . . . An impasta!" He walked up and down the stage as the grumbling resumed. "What do you call a cow with no legs? . . . Ground beef!"

The moans grew in pitch but were unable to hide Jo's booming snort-laugh.

"But seriously, folks"—Mr. Dodd tugged on his suspenders—"I'm so glad you're spending your evening with me and my amazing film class! You're in for a real treat.

"We have six teams of three who will each give an introduction before showing their documentary trailer about the Cascadia Middle School lunchroom. After the last one, you'll text your favorite trailer to the number given at the end.

"Then we'll celebrate the winner in the cafeteria with dessert provided by the cooking club!"

Once the applause died down, Mr. Dodd said, "Please welcome Latesha Evans, Audrey Atkins, and Wilder Pink, otherwise known as the Lunch Squad!"

Olive shifted in her seat. Her dress felt tight.

The first trailer started off with a montage of some fun sightings in Portland. The fifty-foot neon sign of the outline of Oregon with a leaping deer at the top, its red nose lit up for the holidays. A flyer posted on a telephone pole for a missing hen named Kevin. And the annual Portland Stand Up Paddleboard Witches on the Willamette, with hundreds of people dressed as witches paddling with broomsticks. It cut to footage of students at lunch, zooming in on a kid dunking his french fry in chocolate sauce.

"If you think Portland's weird, wait until you see the bizarre food and odd ways kids eat at Cascadia Middle School."

When the trailer ended, Mr. Dodd called the next team onto the stage.

"Everyone's got opinions," one of the kids from the Real Scoop team said. "So we wanted to know what the students at Cascadia thought about their lunchroom.

Please enjoy our trailer for *Spork Up or Spork Down*!"

The closer to their turn, the more jittery Olive got. Her hand kept busy pushing up her glasses, pulling on her sweater, and trying to calm her bouncing knee.

"Next up, the Dream Team! Esme Gold, Jonathon Frank, and Abigail Spencer!"

Olive and Kayla exchanged looks. Rolling her eyes, Kayla mouthed, *Dream Team*. They both covered their mouths to muffle their giggles.

Their team was next.

Olive tried to pay attention, but her thoughts spiraled. Would she have a panic attack? And fall off the stage? To her death? Would exaggerated rumors about her sad, pathetic story be passed down through the decades? Like Fred in the Food Fight of 1988?

The *Cascadia Cliques* trailer wrapped up with a voiceover saying, "Coming to a theater near you." The houselights came up and the auditorium filled with applause. Mr. Dodd ran onto the stage clapping and said, "How about another hand for the Dream Team!"

We're next, we're next, we're next—Olive's heart was pounding—*we're next, we're next!*

"And now for our final trailer, please give a warm welcome for What's Up, Doc!"

Olive swiped away the sweat beading on her forehead.

As she was about to stand up, Kayla leaned in and whispered, "Just speak to me."

Olive gave a small smile.

Following David and Jo, Olive somehow made it down the aisle, up the stairs, and onto the stage. The entire trek she silently repeated, *I'm with my friends. And my friends are with me.*

Chapter Forty-Three

Certified Fresh

THANKS TO THE HOT stage lights, Olive's already-sweaty armpits cranked up to lethal levels. She searched the crowd but couldn't find Kayla.

David began their introduction, just like they'd practiced last night. "As you know, documentaries are films that are supposed to show information that is about something actual, like an event or life story, has no fictional elements, and is based only on facts."

Olive clenched her hands as she waited her turn. A

wiggly figure in front grabbed her attention. She blinked rapidly, then squinted.

Mom? Mom!

Her shoulders loosened.

"What we're about to show is the truth," Jo's voice bellowed, "and surprisingly an Oregon law. But just because something is legal, that doesn't make it right."

Olive stared out into the audience. Even though she couldn't see her best friend's face, she spoke directly to Kayla.

"We think . . ." Her voice squeaked. ". . . what's most important about documentaries is to make a difference. Our goal tonight is to share information. And then it's up to you to take action."

The houselights switched off and David, Jo, and Olive, joined Mr. Dodd in the wing, stage right. Their video began to play.

The screen remained black, layered with the sounds of cheering and stomping. The darkness slowly faded, showing Leevitt the Beaver dancing at the basketball game. A voice-over said, "Meet Oregon's state animal!" and then cut to Waddle lumbering away in the park.

The old lady faded in, waving a frying pan while chasing the beaver. Murmurs rumbled through the crowd. Mr. Dodd inhaled sharply. When the animated Olive dropped into the scene, swinging her lightsaber and blocking the lady's path, the audience cheered.

The reel continued, feeding the audience with tons of beaver facts, the new Oregon bill being introduced to protect beavers, and the petition asking the president to protect all beavers on public land in response to the climate crisis.

The sounds from the crowd kept changing. A gushing "Aw" at kits playing. Gasps when the Busy Beavers CEO announced that it's legal to exterminate the state animal. Hoots and laughter at Leevitt the Beaver moonwalking on the screen.

The words SAVE THE BEAVERS, SAVE THE PLANET faded. Silence hung in the air. Olive sucked in her lips. After several excruciating seconds, the audience began clapping. Olive's shoulders relaxed. She giggled at Mom, wildly waving her arms.

The applause grew, ending in a standing ovation!

Olive couldn't believe it! A rush of adrenaline tingled through her body.

Mr. Dodd jogged onto the stage. "Now, wasn't that an interesting twist?"

He glanced in the team's direction with a puzzled expression but kept going with his usual enthusiasm. "See that number on the screen? Please take out your phones and submit your favorite trailer."

The *Jeopardy!* tune played as Mr. Dodd paced the stage.

Olive beamed. "Thanks for taking this risk with me."

"You know how I like to have my voice heard." Jo smirked. David and Olive laughed.

No matter what happened next, Olive was super proud of her film, her teammates, and herself.

The tune ended. Mr. Dodd waved his hand toward the screen. "The results are in!"

The winning team's name appeared in big block letters: *WHAT'S UP, DOC!*

Clapping, stomping, and hollering flooded the auditorium.

Still backstage, Olive, David, and Jo all stared at one another with wide eyes and squealed. Huddled in a group hug, they jumped up and down. Once they broke apart, Jo said with a fist pump, "We did it!"

"Long live the Oregon beavers!" David cried.

Olive's imagination ran as she pictured their trailer trending on the Rotten Tomatoes website. Scoring high with critics at 94 percent and audiences at 97 percent on the Tomatometer, they would even earn the coveted "Certified Fresh" seal. The critics consensus would read "*Save the Beavers* is a visually engaging and inspiring documentary, taking viewers to emotional heights."

The houselights switched back on. Attendees started filing out.

Mr. Dodd returned.

Olive squeezed her palms back into fists, bracing for the worst.

A big fat F on our project? Kicked out of film class? Suspension?

"Your trailer was amazing, but"—he shook his head—"since you didn't complete the project as assigned, you're disqualified from winning my recommendation for Rose City's film camp."

"We knew there'd be consequences." Jo shrugged. "And we accept them."

David nodded in agreement. "We had to take this opportunity. For the beavers."

Mr. Dodd's head tilted to the side. "Opportunity?"

"When we found out an Oregon House representative was going to be here," David said, "well, it was the only choice."

"Because for us, it was the right choice," Jo said.

"I'm proud of you three." Mr. Dodd grinned. "Fighting for what you believe in. Your trailer achieved exactly what documentaries are supposed to do. Inspire others."

The three shared proud smiles.

A reporter and photographer from the school newspaper poked their heads behind the red velvet curtain. "Can we get some photos and do a quick interview for tomorrow's edition?"

"What's Up, Doc! is all yours!" Mr. Dodd said. "See you guys in the cafeteria when you're done."

"Wait, uh, Mr. Dodd?" Olive bit her lip.

"Yes, Olive?"

"I, um, get why we shouldn't win the personal recommendation, but . . ." She bounced nervously. "I was hoping, uh, could I get a reference letter from you?"

"Of course!" Mr. Dodd said. "I love supporting my students, especially those who show natural talent."

"You totally deserve it," Jo said.

Olive blushed.

As the photographer snapped candid shots, Olive was glad Kayla had picked the itchy dress for her to wear. It might not be the most comfortable, but she looked good in it!

The reporter held out his phone and hit record, "So, who's the brains behind your brave not-about-the-lunchroom trailer?"

David and Jo turned their heads toward Olive. Her face flushed. No one had ever called her brave before.

With a deep exhale, Olive puffed out her chest.

I'm with my friends. And my friends are with me.

"When we found out about the law making it legal to exterminate beavers," Olive said, "we knew we had to do something."

She continued on, proudly explaining why they'd showed the beaver reel instead of their trailer with 99.9 percent confidence.

Chapter Forty-Four

That's All, Folks!

OLIVE TIGHTENED HER HANDS around her sweating glass of water. Her legs felt wobbly after tonight's roller coaster of events. But it wasn't over yet.

The school cafeteria was filled with half the evening assembly's attendees. Desserts lined atop a row of tables along a side wall. All prepared by the cooking club, the selection had an around-the-world theme. Dishes like crunchy British biscuits and chewy American chocolate chip cookies.

Even though she felt great about the audience's response to their reel, and the interview with the school paper, Olive's nerves were too frazzled to eat. Soon Vicky would be introducing them to her mother. An Oregon House representative.

What if Mrs. Goldmann hated our film? What if she laughs? What if everything we did doesn't make a difference?

Mom gave Olive a warm smile.

They stood in a large circle with Kayla, Jo, and David, along with both Jo's and David's parents. It was the first time Olive had noticed that everyone had dressed up. It was also the first time she'd seen Jo in something other than neon or a sports jersey. They looked sharp in a blue button-down, a velvet vest, and black pants. And Kayla sported her most impressive hairstyle yet, gravity-defying braided loops.

"I'm so proud of my kid standing up for what they believe in," Mr. Willems said.

Mrs. Willems shook her head. "Isn't volunteering for Busy Beavers enough?"

"Aw, Mom," Jo whined. "It's not like we released animals from a testing lab!"

"At least no one was hurt." Mr. Willems chuckled.

"Yeah," Jo said, "not like how beavers are being *murdered*."

"I wasn't really shocked with their trailer stunt," said Mrs. Moore. "From being the school mascot to a master at doing surveys, David's obsessed with this goofy-looking rodent."

"Can't blame the kid." Mr. Moore lightly punched David's shoulder. "My wife and I both attended Oregon State and have been taking him to games since he was in diapers."

David's cheeks reddened. "Imagine if they'd gone to University of Oregon. Then I'd be into ducks. And, well, that just seems weird, right?"

Everyone laughed.

"I'm just glad they didn't mention that goo from a beaver's backside," Mom said, making a face.

The group roared.

"Not their backside," Olive managed between giggles. "A gland . . . *near* their butt!"

They were laughing so hard, Mom started to cry, and Olive's throat hurt.

"But seriously"—Mom wiped at her cheeks—"I'm in awe of how talented this one is." She hugged Olive's shoulders. "Just like her dad."

Warmth radiated through her body, as Olive leaned into her mom.

Vicky stepped up next to David and gave a slight wave. "Hey."

"Everyone, this is Vicky." David's cheeks glowed brighter.

Kayla bumped her hip into Olive as Vicky's face began turning from peach to apple-colored.

"And this is my mom." Vicky turned toward the tall, slender woman behind her.

"Mrs. Goldmann." Her mom nodded at the group. She wore a sleek business suit and had an air of no non-sense. Turning her attention to the What's Up, Doc! trio, she said, "Certainly an interesting film shared tonight."

"What's interesting," Jo said, "is that Oregon law making it okay to murder beavers."

Olive was impressed yet saddened that Mrs. Gold-mann didn't even flinch.

"Though residents should be able to defend and

protect their land," Mrs. Goldmann said, "I was outraged seeing that person chasing a beaver with a frying pan. Landowners can trap a problem beaver themselves, but they should hire a wildlife control operator or allow an ODFW-licensed trapper to remove the rodent."

"Murder is murder," Jo huffed, "no matter how the job is done."

"You've made your point," Mr. Willems said, laying a hand on their shoulder. His voice switched to a friendlier tone. "The kids and I volunteer with Busy Beavers, and they often talk about more humane ways to deal with the situation."

"We're the ones taking their homes away from them," David said. "There's got to be a way for humans and beavers to live together peacefully."

"I just have one question," Olive said softly.

Everyone's gaze landed on her. Her chest tightened. Usually, thoughts like hornets would swarm, reminding her to freeze. Though negative chatter still stung in her mind, this was too important. Olive spoke up anyway.

"Why do *you* think the law still exists if there are ways to coexist? Like how we did tonight by increasing the awareness about the benefits of beavers. Especially when it comes to saving the planet."

"Excellent question, Miss . . . ?"

"Olive. Olive Blackwood."

"Well, Miss Blackwood," Mrs. Goldmann said, "sometimes extermination is the quickest and easiest solution, especially when it comes to property damage or flooding. And, of course, money is a factor. We must also consider all Oregon residents, both urban and rural."

Mrs. Goldmann gestured with both hands, emphasizing her point. "A large percentage of Oregon business is agriculture. Damage to those properties affects people's livelihood, causing stress and financial burden to families who've worked on the same lands for generations.

"I've met and personally know many of these families. So while making strides to mitigate climate change is something I agree with, there are other ways of making that happen. We must take into consideration all sides on how to handle problem beavers before changing the law."

Olive nodded. "Thank you, Mrs. Goldmann."

Sure, Olive had read about the destruction of property and flooding that beavers sometimes caused. But

Olive had never considered how saving beavers could potentially hurt families. Maybe there was a way to still save beavers while making sure families weren't negatively affected.

"I don't want anything bad to happen to anybody," Jo said, "but if we don't save our planet, then nobody will have a home. You don't want to be uncomfortable for a little while, at the expense of my livable future?"

"Jo, watch your tone," Mrs. Willems warned.

Olive smiled to herself as the conversation continued.

"I'm going to get something to eat," Olive whispered to Kayla.

"I'll come with."

They excused themselves from the group and snaked their way through the crowd. Olive didn't need to say anything more to Mrs. Goldmann. Jo and David had it under control, and it was pretty obvious that they both enjoyed the spotlight. Olive had said what she wanted to. With her question *and* her film.

If Mrs. Goldmann had heard her, great. If not, Olive was okay with that, too.

Chapter Forty-Five

Olive The Brave

CASCADIA MIDDLE SCHOOL NEWS
SPECIAL EDITION

SAVING BEAVERS SAVES THE PLANET
BY TIMOTHY NETTLES

THE SCHOOL AUDITORIUM WAS PACKED
THURSDAY NIGHT FOR MR. DODD'S
BEGINNING FILM CLASS'S EVENING

ASSEMBLY. THE SHOW ENDED WITH A STANDING OVATION, AND IT WASN'T BECAUSE OF MR. DODD'S GROAN-WORTHY DAD JOKES. SIX TEAMS OF THREE PRESENTED THEIR DOCUMENTARY TRAILERS ABOUT THE SCHOOL LUNCHROOM, EACH TEAM CHOOSING THEIR OWN FOCUS. ONE TEAM, HOWEVER, BROKE THE RULES AND STUNNED THE AUDIENCE WITH A TELL-ALL REEL ABOUT OREGON BEAVERS.

Most students know that beavers are the state animal, and, of course, we all know that our school mascot is Leevitt the Beaver! But did you know that it was legal to "take"—aka kill—beavers in Oregon? And that beavers support other species and help to keep our ecosystem functioning properly?

The brave seventh grader behind this fun, jaw-dropping trailer was Olive Blackwood, an aspiring fantasy film editor. Along with her teammates, Jo

Willems and David Moore, they seized an opportunity to spread the word on how beavers' lives affect ours.

[Candid photograph of Olive, David, and Jo talking and laughing.]

Caption: Olive "the Brave" Blackwood with fellow What's Up, Doc! teammates, David Moore and Jo Willems, in the school auditorium, in the wing, stage right.

"When we lose beavers, we lose so many beaver benefits," said David. "They can turn deserts into wetlands, making homes for birds and mammals. Beavers control water. And water means life."

But not everyone was impressed with What's Up, Doc!'s video. Fellow classmate Abigail Spencer and member of the documentary project group the Dream Team said, "It's unfair to all the other teams. They only won the vote because they didn't follow the rules. That's, like, cheating, right? Who wouldn't choose beavers over the school cafeteria?"

Abigail's teammate Esme Gold, however, commented, "I really enjoyed their film. The editing was top notch."

"There were many reasons why we showed the beaver film instead of our lunchroom trailer," Olive said. "First, there's a new House bill to protect Oregon beavers. The more people who show up in support of the bill at the public hearing next month, the better our chances of saving them.

"But just as important, is letting people know the environmental benefits of beavers when they're able to just live their normal lives. Climate change is happening. And we all know about stuff like recycling. But how many of us know that by saving beavers, we can save our planet?"

"Climate change is scary," Jo chimed

in. "And the law letting people kill beavers is too. But we're scarier. Because kids *can* make a difference."

"Sharing this film is our way of taking action for something that matters," Olive said. "Both for beavers and our future."

Chapter Forty-Six

We Are Family

THE LAST TIME OLIVE and Mom had sat together in the living room, plates piled with pepperoni slices from Pizza Schmizza, was when the local news had reported the beaver found dead in their neighborhood. This time, the television was off as the two gushed about last night's assembly.

"Everybody at school is talking about our reel!" Olive bubbled with glee. "And not just about how much they loved it. So many kids *and* teachers are shocked about that awful Oregon law. A ton of them have signed the petition for the president to protect beavers on public land."

Mom dabbed the corners of her mouth with a napkin. "That's wonderful, honey. I'm so proud of you!"

"Did you really mean what you said last night? About being as good as Dad?"

"Of course! He'd be so proud of you too."

Olive blushed. "I can't wait to start working on my application for the Rose City Summer Film Camp. My short's going to be a silent Halloween dinner, with me and Dad, when—oh no!—we're ambushed by candy corn–eating zombies!"

Mom chuckled, a gleam in her eyes. "That sounds exactly like something your father would make."

Olive straightened in her seat, feeling bigger and stronger.

She continued to talk about her film. About how Kayla and her twin brothers, David, and Jo, were all going to play hungry zombies. And that Kayla, of course, would be doing hair, makeup, and costumes, and choreographing the zombie dance for the scene.

Between Mr. Dodd's reference letter and working with her friends, Olive had a pretty sure shot of getting in. If she didn't, she'd be okay. Sure, she'd be upset. She'd probably even cry. But there'd be future opportunities to apply. And that would give her more time to work on her editing skills. Especially now that her dream was to be an award-winning film editor.

There were several known Black female directors, producers, and writers, like her inspiration, Marsai Martin. But Olive had been excited when she'd learned about Joi McMillon, the first Black woman Oscar nominee for editing. It was proof that Olive's mission was possible.

Olive sighed. "I wish we hung out like this more often."

"I know work takes up a lot of my time," Mom said, "but it's important. For the clients and for us."

Olive nodded. She knew Mom was doing her best and showing up when it mattered most. Like being at the assembly.

"You may not realize this, but all this stuff you've been doing for beavers lately, it's the same as when I'm representing families. We're both fighting for what we believe in."

"Yeah, but . . . I wish you'd fight for our family too."

Mom's face looked pained.

"I will always fight for us." Mom tucked a tuft of hair behind her ear. "And I promise to make more of an effort to spend time with you. So much that you'll start getting sick of me."

Olive shook her head. "Never."

"Since I'll be taking time off work to take you to Dr. Green every week, how about we make it into a playdate?"

Olive's eyebrows squished together.

"Afterward, we could go shopping, to an art gallery, a movie. Whatever you want."

"How about volunteering for Busy Beavers?" Olive buzzed with excitement. "We could get signatures for the petition asking the president to help save beavers."

Mom's nose wrinkled. "You mean like those young adults in front of Trader Joe's?"

"Or we can be detectives for this group called Beavers in Space," she rattled on, "searching satellite imagery for signs of beavers in North America to help with ecosystem restoration!"

"Sure," Mom said. "But maybe we get turns picking the outing."

"Deal!" Olive said. "I've also been thinking about making a short documentary on beavers. Maybe you could help."

Mom wore a sad smile. "Your dad used to ask for my help all the time with his movies."

"He did?" Olive leaned forward.

She nodded, laughing. "I've never been creative with stuff like that, but you know I have no problem sharing my opinion."

Mom paused and stared at the only framed photograph of Dad in the room. His arms were around her pregnant belly. "Your father was incredibly talented."

"I wish you talked about him more."

Mom laid her hand on Olive's cheek. "I used to tell myself that since you received his monthly videos, there was no need for me to bring him up, but . . . honestly, I just wasn't ready. I miss him."

Mom pulled Olive into a tight hug. Olive relaxed into her arms.

Chapter Forty-Seven

That's a Wrap!

OLIVE WINCED AS KAYLA tugged her curls into a tight, high ponytail. Facing the full-length mirror, Olive sat in a chair, watching Kayla doing her hair. Rocking Bantu knots, Kayla hummed along with Jonáe's "Where My Grrrlz Be?"

"I can't believe you chose me to be your date tonight," said Olive.

Kayla's reflection shrugged. "Besties for life, right?"

"But I thought you wanted to go with a group. You know, both girls and guys."

"Nah." Kayla shook her head. "There'll be other dances. I'd rather hang with my girl."

Twitch slunk around a pile of clothes on the floor, skirting quickly past Olive. His silky fur brushed against her bare leg.

"Great picture in the school newspaper, Ms. Olive the Brave." Kayla winked.

Olive witnessed her own face cringe in the mirror.

"Ugh, that quote from Abigail about cheating." Kayla made a face. "Like, she's one to talk after lying to the cocaptains. I'm so annoyed she got the film camp recommendation. She doesn't deserve it."

Olive shrugged. "I'm not worried. She's the one who really needs it."

"Sick burn!" Kayla smirked. "Confident much?"

"Not usually." Olive giggled.

She thought about the conversation in film class from almost a month ago. The one about opinions versus facts. Kayla and her would never know what Abigail had been thinking when she'd told the cocaptains about suspected sabotage. Maybe she'd been lying. Maybe she'd really believed it.

Abigail was entitled to her opinion. But Olive knew the truth.

"Before we move on to makeup"—Kayla waved her blush brush—"how about we consult with the Magic M&M's and Sacred Skittles?"

"Let's do it!" Olive jumped out of the chair. Twitch darted under the bed.

Once they'd settled onto the floor, surrounded by all the necessary supplies, Olive picked up the fun-sized bag of M&M's. She thought about what to ask.

Will I get into Rose City?

Will the Oregon House bill pass?

Will the president issue an executive order to protect beavers on public land?

Will Dr. Green fix my panicky brain?

If what Mom had said that day in the nurse's office was true—"Your feelings are valid, but that doesn't make them a fact"—then maybe Dr. Green *could* help her figure out a way to manage her thoughts. And avoid future panic and diarrhea attacks.

Olive still hated doctors. But Dr. Green wasn't so bad. She'd decided that she wouldn't mind seeing him again. Especially if that meant spending more time with Mom.

Shaking the small bag, Olive focused on her question. "Will somebody ask me to dance tonight?"

Kayla's face brightened with a toothy grin.

Olive tore open the bag and watched as the candies rattled around the plate.

At first, Olive had wanted to know if *she* was going to ask someone to dance. But just thinking about the question had made her feel woozy.

Nope, not gonna ask somebody. And I'm okay with that.

But I can take action in my own way. If Bobby or David or someone else asks me to dance, I'd happily accept. I'm 30, maybe 45 percent sure I'd say yes.

                                        CUT TO:


```
INTERIOR CASCADIA MIDDLE
SCHOOL GYM. LATER THAT
EVENING.


The latest Beyoncé hit
blares. Kayla, Jo, David,
```

Vicky, and Kayla's dance
team friends, Heather and
April, are dancing and
laughing together. We see
all different types of
students dancing around
them.

ANGLE ON OLIVE. Alone by the
bleachers feeling lonely.

Kayla and Jo arrive.

                KAYLA
     Dance with us!

Olive shakes her head.

                JO
     This isn't a request.
     Mean Vegan Jo orders you
     onto the dance floor.

Olive reluctantly takes Kayla's outstretched hand. Kayla and Jo drag Olive to the dance floor and join their friends still dancing. Kayla and Jo immediately start dancing. Olive stands outside the group, watching. David smiles at Olive. Olive smiles back.

Kayla leans into Olive.

                    KAYLA
     See? It's not so bad. Not
     when you're with friends.

Olive looks at her friends. She slowly smiles.

ANGLE ON KAYLA, HEATHER, AND APRIL doing pop-and-lock moves.

ANGLE ON JO, DAVID, AND
VICKY and their silly dance
moves.

BACK TO OLIVE.

Olive moves into the middle
of the group and breaks into
a funky dance. Her friends
cheer her on.

> OLIVE (VOICE-OVER)
> Yup, that's me dancing.
> Can you believe that
> I'm actually busting
> a move? In public? And
> yeah, I know what you're
> thinking. I'm a horrible
> dancer. And, well, you
> wouldn't be wrong. And
> you know what else?

ANGLE ON BOBBY dancing
awkwardly with his friends.

BACK TO OLIVE still dancing
just as awkwardly.

> OLIVE (VOICE-OVER)
> It isn't so bad.
> (beat)
> Not when you're with
> friends.

Pull back to REVEAL BOBBY
walking over to Olive and
asking her to dance.

ZOOM IN ON OLIVE'S ELATED
FACE. Nothing for a few
beats. She nods yes.

ANGLE ON OLIVE AND BOBBY
awkwardly dancing together.

ANGLE ON KAYLA bouncing
around with excitement. She
mouths *OMG! The M&M's were
right!* Unable to read lips,
Olive is confused. Kayla
makes the heart hand sign.
Olive is all smiles.

We watch as Bobby's friends
join Olive, Bobby, and all
her friends. They're all
dancing and having fun.

> OLIVE (VOICE-OVER)
> My best friend, Kayla,
> and I always do our best
> to follow the rules of
> magic. One of those
> rules, and my favorite,
> is that Magic Is Stronger
> When Done Together. Magic
> is the unexplainable,

sometimes unimaginable,
but undeniable truth.
Magic is real. I believe
in magic. I believe in
myself. . . .

ANGLE ON OLIVE.

OLIVE (VOICE-OVER)
Because I'm with my
friends, and my friends
are with me.

OLIVE WINKS at all of us with
a warm smile.

FADE OUT:

THE END.

(CREDITS ROLL TO "WHERE MY
GRRRLZ BE?" by JONÀE.)

Author's Note

Even though *Olive Blackwood Takes Action!* is a work of fiction, a lot was based on real life.

Like Olive, I too suffer from anxiety and had once had a panic attack in public. I've learned over the years that in order to show up in the world, I must do it in my own way and in my own time. I wanted to tell a story starring someone who wants to speak up but often doesn't know how to move past the fear.

I also love animals. When I saw a friend reading a nonfiction book about how beavers can save the planet, I was curious. So I started doing research. I've never seen or heard about someone chase, harm, or kill a beaver with a frying pan. But for some weird reason, that's what I first pictured when I'd learned about the Oregon law allowing residents to "take"—aka kill—the state animal. Once I knew the main character and that her journey was to learn how she could use her voice to help save beavers, that's when the story began to take life.

I don't have all the answers when it comes to activism. But I do know that it's important to learn and talk about stuff that matters. It can be overwhelming when we hear about all the things harming our planet, communities, and those places, people, and things we care about. I often feel like my own "small" actions won't make a difference, so why bother? And I could never imagine filing a first-of-its-kind climate case against a state like the young environmental activists mentioned by Jo in Chapter Twenty (something that really happened and where a judge sided with the Montana youths!). But *every* action—big and small—affects change, often in ways we may never know. So I try to do whatever I can, whenever I can.

If you're interested in taking action for something you believe in, learn more about the issue. One of the best resources for research is your local library. From books to online tools, librarians have always helped guide me to reliable sources. A great way to take action is to get involved with or support local organizations that work in your area of interest. Often, many national organizations have local or regional chapters. There are many ways to contribute, so find out how *you* want to make a difference. Every action counts!

I also don't have all the answers when it comes to living a full life while anxious and/or depressed. But I do know that you're not alone. I often wanted to give up because I didn't believe I was worthy of being loved and that my voice didn't matter.

If you or someone you love is struggling with anxiety or depression, then please reach out to a parent, a teacher, or a trusted loved one. It took me a long time to ask for help, and the only reason I did was because someone who cared about me asked if I needed it. You matter.

Writing is my passion. Though it's often a solitary activity, writers must be vulnerable and put themselves out there if they want their stories read. The same may be true for whatever you want to experience in life. My hope is that no matter your fear, this story will inspire you to make your own path and create boundaries to work toward your goals and dreams, one step at a time.

Everyone has a voice. Every voice matters. You get to choose how and when to use it.

Acknowledgments

I'm forever grateful to my amazing agent, Ronald Gerber. Thank you for always being a great sounding board and champion of my work.

Thank you to my brilliant editor, Aly Heller, and to the incredible team behind this book at Aladdin. And a huge thanks to Tiara Iandiorio for the cover design and to the incredibly talented Simone Douglas for the gorgeous cover art.

This book wouldn't be if it wasn't for my wonderful writing community. A huge shout out to my early readers for your awesome feedback—Curtis Chen, Carolyn O'Doherty, Shawn Peters, and Nancy Tandon. And to all my writing pals and friends that keep me sane, especially Vannessa McClelland, Kelly Garrett, Cat Winters, Jenn Reese, Elaina Brown, Gracia Kai, Dawn Loehlein, Lisa Nabipour, and Camden Campe-Simpson.

I'm so grateful to all the teachers, librarians,

bookstagrammers, and readers who've supported me and my work. And a special thank you to Audrey Truesdale who helped me realize my worth.

Thank you to all the wonderful people for their time and assistance during my research on Oregon beavers: Joe Liebezeit at Portland Audubon; Molly Honea at Think Wild Central Oregon; Danielle Moser at Oregon Wild; Sunriver Nature Center & Observatory; the Oregon Zoo; and Johnson Creek Watershed Council. Thank you to my magical Portland family and fellow advocates in saving Mother Earth: Lynn, Diana, Nessa, Ron, and Elizabeth. And a huge thank you and shout out to the most adorable, hard-working keystone species ever: the beaver.

Much love to my family: my mom, Lydia Thomas; Fred Thomas; Libby Rejman; Mary VanSandt; Colleen McCarrig; Oakley; and my partner for life, Mike McCarrig.

Mike, thanks so much for your unwavering support and belief in me and my storytelling dreams. With you by my side, I know everything magical is possible.

About the Author

Sonja Thomas writes stories for readers of all ages, often featuring brave, everyday girls doing extraordinary things. Her debut novel, *Sir Fig Newton and the Science of Persistence* is an Oregon Book Award finalist, an Oregon Spirit Book Award Honor recipient, a Washington State Book Award finalist, and a Bank Street Best Children's Book selection. She's also a contributing author for *Good Night Stories for Rebel Girls: 100 Real-Life Tales of Black Girl Magic*. Raised in Central Florida, and a Washington, DC, transplant for eleven years, she's now "keeping it weird" in the Pacific Northwest.

Visit her online at BySonjaThomas.com.